THE CRYSTAL OF MEDORA

THE CRYSTAL OF MEDORA

THE MIRRORED CROWN: BOOK TWO

JESSICA R. LEMORE

ISBN- 13: 978-1-7353962-3-1 (Paperback)

ISBN-13: 978-1-7353962-5-5 (Hardback)

ISBN-13: 978-1-7353962-4-8 (E-Book)

For my son, Nello. May you never struggle to find your purpose in this world.

CONTENTS

1

THE PAPERS

Lana threw the papers to the ground. She shut her eyes and listened to the pendulum on the grandfather clock as it swayed from side to side—the gentle tick mocking her, reminding her that she was running out of time. She had found the papers two weeks ago in Poklin's Variety Store, before her uncle, King Ramos, closed the shop. Poklin had finally admitted his role in the Rebellion. Alderic was now in hiding, plotting his rise to power.

She reopened her eyes and rubbed her forehead in frustration, hoping to soothe the headache that hovered on the edges of her consciousness. She knew the papers could have no significance, but had no other leads on the Crystal either. She had her chance at destroying the rebels' greatest weapon but had been too scared of the demons inside.

She looked around her bedroom, searching for a distraction, something to keep her mind off the papers. While her bedroom was nice, it still didn't feel like hers. It seemed as if she was in someone else's room, living someone else's life. Unfortunately, the only thing that caught her attention was the crisp white paper underneath the trunk at the foot of her bed.

Lana bent down to retrieve it, placing her hand on the trunk for balance, her gaze drifting to the dragons and sea serpents etched onto the wood. When the paper was safely in her grip, she stood up, searching for the other. A moment later, she saw it near one of the bookshelves. She slowly made her way to it, passing the enormous bed and dresser.

She studied the papers again, looking for clues, anything that would tell her why the rebels had them in the first place. They were hand-drawn blueprints. Both looked to be the same size and had a few notes in the margins, labeling different parts of the room. The only noticeable difference was the layout.

The first drawing had one entrance that opened into a large room. The area to the right was labeled *desk*. Straight ahead of the entrance was another box labeled *restroom* and next to that, to the left, was another doorway, which was circled in pencil. The rest of the room was empty, except for a handful of hastily drawn squares that puzzled her.

The second drawing was sparser than the first. The only entrance was on the far wall, opposite the first sketch. In this drawing, the area to the left was labeled *desk*. To the right of the entrance was a tiny room. Beyond that, the paper was blank.

She studied the handwriting again, trying to find any resemblance to the handwriting of someone she knew. She had already deduced that the same person had drawn both pictures. The words were printed in a tall, scribbled script. It looked as if they were drawn in a hurry, perhaps as an afterthought.

They plagued her. She couldn't stop looking at them, trying to decipher their secrets. She rubbed her hand across the parchment, feeling the familiar texture once again. What surprised her was that it reminded her of paper from Mt. Sinclair.

She twirled her ring around her finger, trying to think like a rebel. Someone had sketched the buildings for a reason. She knew they were important, but why? Were they the rebels' hideouts? If so, where were they located? She wanted to show them to King Ramos and her parents but didn't trust her uncle's advisor, Damarius Pilkins.

When Lana had been captured by rebels, Damarius had been with them, leading them. After she escaped, she had been told that it was all an act. Damarius had infiltrated the rebels years ago in order to bring back information. She didn't believe it though. A shiver passed through her as she remembered Damarius leading the group of rebels to the graveyard.

She turned to the grandfather clock, watching the pendulum while processing her thoughts. It was her favorite thing about the bedroom as it contained a secret only a handful of people knew—it held an underground passage to the forest surrounding the castle. A moment later, she turned from the clock, looking at the few possessions from her previous life in Mt. Sinclair that decorated the room. Pictures, candles, and various knickknacks lined the bookshelves, while jeans and T-shirts hid in the dresser.

Not even a month ago, Lana had been a ninth-grade student at Mt. Sinclair High School in Mt. Sinclair, New York. She enjoyed her simple life of chores, school, and homework. She had two best friends, Ava Graham and Trevor McAllister.

All that changed the day she was attacked. She had been walking home from school through Frazier Woods when she was ambushed by two men. Soon after, she learned that her whole life had been an elaborate facade, orchestrated to keep her safe from her murderous birth father, Alderic, and his band of rebels. Her birth mother, Kalinia, had been murdered fifteen years ago when Lana was only a few months old. To top it off, she was from another dimension and a princess of Bridian. The people she had grown to believe were her parents were only guardians, assigned to keep her safe. She still considered Grayson and Jacqueline her parents though. They had raised her, and she couldn't imagine her life without them.

She hid the papers in the trunk and placed her crown on her head. While it was beautiful, she felt awkward wearing it. Her stomach rumbled, and she knew it was time for lunch. When she opened her bedroom door, she saw Grant, one of the soldiers assigned to guard her, pacing before it. He stopped walking, standing at attention.

She was glad that Grant was still assigned to her. She hadn't felt that way at first. Having a guard made her stand out when all she wanted to do was fit into her new home. But since the Crystal disappeared, and Alderic still searched for her, she felt safe knowing she had protection when she needed it.

"I'm going to the dining hall."

"About time, I'm starving."

She tried to smile but was too worried to make it look convincing. Her lips immediately sank into a frown.

"What's wrong?" he asked.

"I feel like I made everything worse," she said. "I just really want life to go back to how it was before. I miss Mt. Sinclair. I miss my friends. I still can't believe I lost the Crystal. I had my chance to destroy it and failed."

Grant nodded. "It's not your fault. If you had destroyed it, the demons probably would have killed you."

"I know," she lied, closing the bedroom door behind her.

She had told the lie for so long now it was beginning to sound like she actually believed it. She blamed herself for losing the Crystal. She had it, was holding it in her hands, but didn't know how to destroy it. The last thing she remembered was it falling from her hands. As much as it pained her, she didn't see who picked it up, and there had been no news of Alderic or Contlay since. She didn't even know if her cousin Damon, who had joined the rebel faction, was still alive.

It hurt to think of Contlay. He had led her to believe he was on her side, looking out for her. Too late, she learned he had always been a rebel. Nothing had ever made her feel so betrayed.

She silently made her way through the empty hallway. She still couldn't believe she was a princess and lived in the enormous castle. A part of her wished she could go back to Mt. Sinclair and resume her ordinary teenage life, away from Alderic. She didn't have a royal bone in her body. How could she ever be Queen of Bridian? How was she supposed to rule a kingdom?

She wondered if the castle would ever truly feel like home. At first glance, Bridian didn't seem much different than Mt. Sinclair, but the longer she spent in her new home, the more differences she found. There were no phones, computers, or even cars. But, at least, there was electricity.

When she stepped into the enormous dining hall, she saw that she was one of the last to arrive. She listened to the happy conversation buzzing around her. It seemed as if everyone had forgotten that just a few short weeks ago Alderic had overtaken Bridian. Even though Ramos had regained the throne, the Crystal was missing. She knew it would only be a matter of time before the demons were released.

Lana's eyes swept the room to look for her parents, knowing they would have saved her usual seat between them. Sure enough, there was an empty plate lying between their full ones. She walked the length of the hall to join them. When her uncle saw her pass, he discreetly shook his head from side to side, silently confirming that the Crystal had not been found.

After she sat down, she sipped her water, flinching when the cold liquid hit her throat. She set the glass down and saw her cousin Dominic watching her, almost as if he was waiting for her to look at him.

He leaned across the table and whispered, "I've been thinking about the papers. I know who can help us."

She nodded, urging him to continue.

A slight grin crossed his lips before he said, "The Outcasts."

2

THE PLAN

Lana ate very little at lunch. Her mind was buzzing with thoughts of how she was going to find the Outcasts. She knew it wouldn't be easy, and even if she happened to find them again, she wondered if they would help. They had once been rebels. As punishment for betraying Alderic, they were banished from the Rebellion and cursed into becoming hideous monsters.

"Do you think they'll help us?" Dominic asked.

She shrugged. "I don't know. It's the only idea we've come up with in two weeks though."

"Lana, aren't you hungry?" Jacqueline asked.

At the interruption, Dominic took a sip of his Choclochino. Lana looked at her own drink and sighed, too nervous to eat or drink anything.

"I ate the fruit," she answered.

Jacqueline sighed loudly. "You need to eat more than the fruit."

Dominic giggled at their exchange and Lana envied him. His parents sat at the head of the table. They weren't watching their children, monitoring the amount of food left on their plates. While she loved her parents, she didn't like the constant supervision.

She pushed a strand of curly brown hair behind her ear. Most of the conversation centered around the rainy weather that had beset the kingdom during the last week. Others were talking about the empty shops in the Square, wagering what would replace Poklin's Variety Shop.

Jacqueline leaned back in her chair and reached for Grayson's hand. Lana had recently learned her parents weren't married and had only been pretending to be a couple for their cover in Mt. Sinclair. When they saw that she was watching, they dropped each other's hands. She wondered if they missed the charade.

"Dominic!" Deliah said. "That was mine! You took it right off my plate."

Lana looked at her cousins. They were fighting, again. She knew no others that could carry on a fight as they did. One thing she realized after spending so much time with them was that fighting was their strange way of communicating. They usually weren't big arguments, just heated discussions.

"It was on my plate," Dominic taunted, biting a buttery biscuit and waving it before his sister. "It's mine!"

"That's enough," Ramos called from the head of the table. "Deliah, there are other biscuits."

"But that one was mine!" Deliah answered but was effectively silenced by the no nonsense look on her father's face.

Ramos went back to his conversation with his advisor, Damarius, ignoring his daughter. Lana wished she could hear what they were talking about. Was Damarius prying information from Ramos to bring back to the rebels?

Across the table, Deliah and Dominic continued to argue over the biscuit, albeit silently to avoid their father's stern gaze. Lana could easily pass as their sibling. They shared the same brown eyes and curly hair. Deliah even had a tiny freckle above her left eyebrow, same as Lana.

She looked around the room. Terris was at the next table, talking to Marnie. He had become a good friend. They had gone through so much in such a short period of time, it felt as if they had known each other forever.

Kiernan was sitting next to Marnie. His wavy brown hair fell into his face but he brushed it away, revealing his bright blue eyes. When he looked up at her, she immediately turned away, embarrassed at having been caught staring. It was safe to say she had a crush on him. Her stomach flip-flopped every time she saw him.

"Can you talk to Nick tonight?" Grayson asked. "He's not taking things very well."

Lana searched the room again. Mrs. Jacobs and Nick hadn't joined them. Three days ago they had left Mt. Sinclair for Bridian and were now staying in the castle. Mr. Jacobs would soon join them. She still couldn't believe that her next door neighbors in Mt. Sinclair were also from Bridian.

"I'd rather not."

The last thing she wanted to do was talk to Nick. They hadn't gotten along, primarily because he made it his life's mission to torment her. When her father stood, she realized he hadn't heard her, or had chosen to ignore her remark.

She put her elbow on the table, cradling her head in the palm of her hand as she continued to push the food around her plate. She tried clearing her head. She was hoping if she stopped thinking about the drawings their significance would just come to her. When that didn't work, she tried talking to Deliah and Dominic, but they had moved on from their fight about the biscuit and were now glaring at each other icily.

When lunch was over, she followed her cousins to the room on the third floor that overlooked Bridian Square. It had become their regular meeting place. Terris had joined them and silently walked beside her, lost in thought as well. Lana made a beeline to the window and looked out at the Square. It had begun raining again, and she watched those down below run into the shops surrounding the fountain, looking for shelter from the deluge. She sat on the couch, thankful that Grant was in the hallway, giving them a little privacy. Before she could tell Terris their plan, he surprised them with his own.

"I'm going to find my parents."

The room remained silent. Deliah and Dominic looked at Lana, urging her to take the lead.

"Why?" she asked. "Terris, they abandoned you."

"Not the kind of parents I'd want," Dominic added.

"It's something I have to do," he said. "I want to ask them why... why they didn't love me."

While she couldn't understand why he wanted to find the people that had offered him up as a sacrifice to the demons, she understood his need for answers. When she had been told that Jacqueline and Grayson weren't her parents, she wanted to learn everything she could about her birth parents, the good and the bad.

"I know my dad's in the Yards," he said. "I don't know if I can visit him."

"You can't visit anyone in the Yards," Dominic said. "I've asked Dad before. I would love to go. I can't wait to be a reaper one day!"

Lana wondered what it was like in the Bone Yards. She knew it must be horrible. Bonawickham Yards, more commonly referred to as the Bone Yards, was a dimension that served as a prison for the worst criminals. Her birth father, Alderic, had recently escaped the prison with the help of Damon, her cousin who was now missing. Reapers were hired by the Council of Elders, the advisors for the different dimensions. Their job was to find criminals and escort them to prison.

"I'll have to find my mom then," Terris said, looking out the window again.

She knew his mom was in hiding, along with the rest of the rebels. Lana didn't understand how his mom could so easily give up her son. The rain had intensified, and she watched the water trickle down the window in long lines.

"I don't think it's a good idea," Deliah said.

"Yeah, I don't understand why you'd want anything to do with them," Dominic added.

Terris looked at his feet. "You wouldn't understand. You have parents that love you. You're royalty, your lives are perfect."

Deliah rolled her eyes. "My life's not perfect. I still have to go to lessons."

Lana smiled at her younger cousin's naivety. A change of subject was in order; she would talk to Terris alone.

"How are we going to find the Outcasts?"

Dominic filled Terris in on his idea, whispering so Grant wouldn't hear. Lana listened to the rain, her eyes growing heavy. Ever since the fateful night she lost the Crystal, she hadn't been sleeping much.

"What's the plan for actually finding them?" Terris asked.

"That's for someone else to figure out." Dominic rolled his eyes. "I can't be responsible for everything."

"Do you think those books are still in Damon's room?" Terris asked, remembering when Lana found a few books on black magic in his bedroom. "There has to be something about the Outcasts in one of them."

Deliah scoffed. She didn't believe her brother had joined the Rebellion. It was hard for Lana to believe as well, even though she hadn't known him very long. She couldn't understand why someone would want to help Alderic, why someone would willingly join a person who wanted to release demons into the world for personal gain.

"Can you check his room later?"

Dominic stood from the couch and took his sister's arm, pulling her up. "We might as well go now."

Deliah reluctantly followed him. When they were gone, Terris turned to Lana. He raised his eyebrow in question. She knew what he was thinking, but he said it anyway.

"That's the plan?"

"It's better than nothing."

"Have you talked to Nick yet?" he asked, pulling at a stray piece of thread on his cloak.

Although Terris had inherited a substantial amount of money from his uncle, Alexander, he still wore his old cloaks. He bought new ones, along with a lot of candy and toys from Poklin's but felt guilty using them. He hid everything he bought in a trunk, refusing to touch it. She couldn't blame him. Two weeks ago they learned that Alexander was still alive, a slave to the rebels.

"No."

"You're going to have to sooner or later."

"I know." She sighed. "I still can't believe that he's here. He made my life miserable in Mt. Sinclair, and I know he's going to do the same here."

"People change."

"I know you think your parents have. Try not to be too disappointed when you find out they haven't."

She twirled a strand of hair around her finger, trying to keep her mind off Mt. Sinclair. After a few minutes of awkward silence, Lana lay on the couch and closed her eyes, listening to the rain hit the window. She wondered what Ava and Trevor were up to. Did they even miss her?

Thoughts of Mt. Sinclair turned to the Outcasts. She remembered meeting them a few weeks ago. They believed Lana would have the power to change them back, to reverse Alderic's curse. Even though she knew they needed their help deciphering the papers, she wasn't sure she wanted to incur that particular debt. She didn't think she would ever be powerful enough to take away the curse and didn't want the obligation.

They sat in a comfortable silence. When she heard her cousin's voices in the hall she sat up just in time to see them burst into the room.

"All his books were gone," Dominic said, collapsing on a chair.

"Dad must have taken them," Deliah added.

Lana wasn't surprised. She had told her uncle that she found Alderic's journal amongst Damon's books, so it was only natural that he would have confiscated the rest.

"I guess we need to find another way to the Outcasts," Dominic said.

"Why is this so difficult!" Lana said. "I've been pouring over those papers for days and still, nothing. I wish someone would tell me what they are."

She balled her hands into fists and pressed them into her thighs, blinking back the tears.

"I bet it's their hideout," Dominic said.

"Maybe they're just random drawings," Deliah added. "They might not even be important."

"I know they're important. Why else would they have been in the rebels' meeting room at Poklin's?"

"They were left behind," Deliah countered, pulling her hair into a ponytail. "If they were important, they would have taken them."

"Maybe we should look at them again. Something new might come to us," Terris said.

She didn't need to look at the papers. She had been studying them for so long they were imprinted into her memory, taunting her.

"What we should be planning is how we're going to find the Outcasts. We're wasting time looking at them."

"I think finding them will be easy," Terris said.

Lana stared at her friend, silently urging him to continue. His green eyes twinkled as he ran his hand through his hair.

"Well, are you going to tell us?" Dominic asked.

"How did we find them last time?"

"We didn't," she answered. "They found us."

"Exactly," he said. "All we have to do is walk around the forest. They'll come to us."

She wasn't sure it was going to be that easy. The forest scared her. She didn't want to know what other creatures it held besides the fairies and Shadow Splinters.

"He's right," Dominic said a moment later. "They found us once, they'll find us again."

Lana bit her lip, wondering if the Outcasts would know what the drawings were. "I should finish my homework. Let's meet after dinner."

"You still haven't finished?" Terris asked. "What are you writing about?"

"Manifestation. I don't get it. How can you make something happen by just believing it?"

"Well, with that attitude it's no wonder you're having problems," he laughed. "Did you read the assignment on alternate timelines?" When she shook her head, he added, "I'll help you."

Deliah stood with a dramatic sigh. "I suppose I should work on my paper too."

As they made their way to their bedrooms, Lana had an idea. She ran past her cousins, making her way to a familiar hall that she hadn't seen in two weeks, since the Crystal disappeared. She paused when she reached a painted mirror displaying a weeping willow tree leaning over a peaceful lake. A slight tremble passed through her. She took a deep breath and touched the mirror. Nothing happened. She pushed harder and the mirror moved, sliding to the right and coming off balance.

Behind her, Grant laughed. "That's been sealed."

The only way she was going to get into the abandoned hall again was by asking Ramos, but something told her that wouldn't work. She was contemplating her options when she heard a voice she wished she hadn't.

"Lana," Mrs. Jacobs called. "How nice to see you again. You too, Terris."

She knew her luck had been too good to be true. She had escaped Nick for three whole days. She was bound to see him eventually.

Mrs. Jacobs was wearing a black lace shirt and dark blue jeans. Her blonde hair was curled, and her long nails were painted red. Her makeup was perfect. Lana wondered why she had gone through all the trouble to get dressed up just to roam around the castle.

"Hi," Lana muttered, trying to think of an excuse to leave before Nick joined them. "We won't bother you. You probably have a lot of unpacking left."

Mrs. Jacobs smiled. "Don't be silly. Please, come in. I was just talking to Nick." When she saw Deliah and Dominic her face lit up. "You're Queen Charlotte's children!"

The siblings remained silent and watched her curiously.

"I'm friends with your mother," she explained. "At least I was until I had to move."

Nick mumbled something from inside the bedroom. Mrs. Jacobs glared as her son appeared.

"Come say hello."

Nick stepped into the hallway. He was taller than Lana. He was wearing blue jeans and a dark-blue Mt. Sinclair High School sweatshirt. He looked tired, as if he hadn't slept in days.

"What do you want?"

She hadn't seen Nick so despondent before. He hadn't even

called her Laughs, his nickname for her in Mt. Sinclair. Nick thought it was perfect because it incorporated the action many people felt after spending time with her and her family.

"Come in," Mrs. Jacobs said, pushing Nick back into the bedroom and looking at Deliah and Dominic happily. "How's your mother?"

"We don't know," Dominic said. "She's been gone awhile."

"Where is she?" Mrs. Jacobs asked with an air of concern coloring her tone.

"With our aunt," Deliah answered. "That's what Dad told us."

"Well, this is my son, Nick," Mrs. Jacobs said, turning to Grant. "It's nice to see you again."

"Margaret," Grant said, extending his hand. "It's nice to see you too."

"You're still with the army?" she asked, looking at his blue cloak with the tiny gold and purple crest on the left lapel.

"I've been assigned to guard Princess Lana."

Nick kicked the duffel bag by his feet and said, "I hate it here."

Lana didn't want to anger him, so she looked away, studying the room. It was large, with an enormous bed and beautiful mahogany chests. Two designer suitcases lay on the floor, clothes spilling out of them.

"We're taking our time settling in." Mrs. Jacobs picked up a shirt and folded it. "Nick will start lessons with you tomorrow. King Ramos was kind enough to let us stay here until we find our own place in Bridian."

"I want to go back to Mt. Sinclair," Nick complained. "I want to go home."

The air was heavy. Her friends were looking at the floor. She knew they were just as uncomfortable as she was.

"We already went over this," Mrs. Jacobs said between clenched teeth.

"When is Mr. Jacobs coming?" Lana asked, trying to break the tension.

Mrs. Jacobs busied herself with unpacking her suitcases. "In a few days. He has to finish some things in Mt. Sinclair."

"Don't lie," Nick said. "He's not coming, I know he's not."

"Your father has to tie up a few loose ends. That's all."

"He said he hates it here." Nick crossed his arms over his chest. "And I do too. I want to go home."

Mrs. Jacobs turned to Terris. "Have they found Alexander?"

Terris shook his head. Mrs. Jacobs frowned. Nick rolled his eyes.

"Why do you care? Who is he to you anyway?" he asked.

Mrs. Jacobs moved closer to her son. "He was a good friend."

Nick laughed. "He's all you talk about lately. You talk about him more than Dad."

"Not now," Mrs. Jacobs said between clenched teeth, eyeing her son sharply.

Nick crossed his arms over his chest, glaring defiantly at his mother. "I don't want to be here. I don't understand why you don't seem to care about Dad anymore. All you talk about is that other guy."

Lana was about to intervene, to tell them she would come back another time, when Mrs. Jacobs blurted out, "I was engaged to Alexander. It was a long time ago. Before I married your father."

Nick glared at his mother before pushing Lana out of his way and storming into the hall. No one said anything, not even Grant. Lana remembered when Mrs. Jacobs had learned her friend's last name in Mt. Sinclair. It looked as if she had seen a ghost. Lana now knew why the name had struck a nerve.

"It was a very long time ago," Mrs. Jacobs said.

A soldier ran past the room in a hurry. Almost as an

afterthought, he doubled back, stopping at the door, ignoring everyone but Lana. He bowed.

"Queen Charlotte has returned. She wants to see you."

"Mom's here?" Deliah squealed. "Where is she?"

The soldier cleared his throat. "She only asked to see Princess Lana."

"She's our mother," Dominic said, stomping his foot.

Lana looked at her cousins, her heart almost breaking when she saw their sad faces. Her aunt was horrible to her children. She looked at the ground, studying the floor. She didn't want to see their disappointed faces again.

Terris caught her gaze and smiled weakly. Lana followed the soldier into the hall, upset on behalf of her cousins but eager to find out what Charlotte wanted.

3

———

CHARLOTTE'S RETURN

The only thing Lana heard was the sound of their feet on the stone floor. She couldn't believe her aunt didn't want to see her children after being apart for close to three weeks. She remembered Charlotte's nonchalance when Damon had disappeared, before King Ramos's birthday, and suddenly her behavior wasn't as shocking. Was Ramos even aware she had returned?

When they stepped into an unfamiliar hall, she turned to make sure Grant was still behind her.

"What does Queen Charlotte want with Princess Lana?" he asked.

The soldier was young, at least younger than the other soldiers she had seen at the castle. He had very short black hair and green eyes. His mouth was framed by a trimmed goatee.

"I don't know," he answered. "I was stationed outside the castle when she arrived. She gave Gerard her horse and asked me to find Princess Lana."

Having said his piece, he looked forward again, his long cloak billowing behind him. Lana's mind raced. Why did her aunt want to speak to her in such a hurry?

"Where are we going?"

The soldier stopped walking. "I'm sorry. I should have told you. I also should have introduced myself."

Lana was unable to follow what the soldier was saying. Her hands had started to tingle; she curled them into a ball, trying to distract herself from the feeling. Ever since the night she lost the Crystal, she had felt off—she experienced a strange prickling in her hands and she had frequent headaches. She told herself it was only stress, but she was starting to question if anxiety was the culprit and wondered if she should tell her parents in case the cause was something more sinister.

"My name's Ander," he said. "I'm taking you to the King and Queen's private chambers. Queen Charlotte is waiting for you there."

"It's nice to meet you," she said, regaining her composure.

"Ander is one of our youngest soldiers," Grant said.

"I am the youngest," Ander added, his lips curving into a boyish smile. "By four months. I turned 18 two months ago."

Lana and Grant followed him to a staircase. Two soldiers were standing guard outside the entrance. When they saw Grant, they nodded solemnly.

Ander led them inside the stairwell. The stairs climbed up in a circle and were lined in red velvet. Beautiful paintings hung on the wall. They were in one of the castle's many turrets. She wished she had more time to look at the pictures, but Ander was urging her to keep up.

When she stepped off the last stair she looked around the enormous room. It was the biggest bedroom she had ever seen. She realized it was about the size of the whole ground floor of her house in Mt. Sinclair.

A gigantic bed was set in the middle of the room underneath a beautiful chandelier etched with flowers. Two dressers stood on either side of the bed and a third was behind it, facing the far wall. A built-in bookshelf, brimming with books, was at the back. A trunk, like the one in her bedroom, lay at the foot of the bed. She counted four windows, each framed by dark-red curtains tied with gold cords. Two oversized chairs sat to their left. Clothes and jewelry were piled on them. Charlotte seemed to be in the middle of unpacking.

"I heard you were in Sumner," an icy voice said.

Charlotte emerged from a door to the right, her cold blue eyes narrowed. Her long blonde hair was tied in an elaborate bun, and her gold crown looked like it had been recently polished. At first, Lana didn't understand what her aunt meant. Then she remembered. When she and Terris had escaped the rebels, they passed through a little town called Sumner.

"We didn't stay very long. How did you know we were there?" Lana was confused. She didn't know why her aunt even cared she had been in Sumner. Of all the things she had done in the past few weeks, she was surprised this was what Charlotte wanted to talk about.

Charlotte stepped closer to her niece. The energy in the room shifted. Hot air wrapped around her, almost suffocating her.

"I know what you were doing."

Charlotte's tone shocked her. It was filled with venom. Lana looked at Grant and saw that he was whispering to Ander. A moment later, the young soldier left the room in a hurry.

"I don't understand. We weren't there very long. We were on our way to the castle, to find the Crystal."

"You're very nosy," her aunt snapped.

"I don't understand," she repeated, still clueless. She furrowed her eyebrows, her hands limp at her sides. "I didn't do anything wrong."

Charlotte erupted into a wicked laugh, sending chills down her spine. Lana took an involuntary step back, her flaccid arms now taut with fret.

"My sister told me all about your visit." Charlotte stepped

closer, bridging the gap between them. "She didn't know it was you though."

"I didn't realize you were related to them," Lana said, the family's names on the tip of her tongue. "They were nice. They invited us to eat with them."

"They didn't know who you were."

"How did you know we visited them if they didn't know who we were?" Lana asked, finally recalling their names—Henry, Madge, Karla, Nadia, and Ned.

"Madge told me that they had a pair of strange visitors," Charlotte turned her back to her, whether to hide her anger, Lana couldn't tell, "who had just appeared from the woods and were in a hurry to get to Bridian. I thought this was peculiar, so I prodded. She described you perfectly, as well as that boy Ramos took in."

Henry had mentioned Madge having a family in Bridian. Lana remembered thinking that Madge looked like her aunt, but was still surprised to learn the truth. Charlotte walked to the bed and pushed the loose hair from her face before picking up a diamond and emerald necklace, inspecting it closely.

"Well, now you know my secret. You should have told them who you were instead of trying to hide the truth."

Ramos burst into the room. "Charlotte. When did you get back?"

"Moments ago," she answered, tossing the necklace to the bed. "I've only been unpacking."

He looked confused. "What did you need Lana for?"

"We were just talking. About the importance of honesty."

She heard more commotion in the direction of the stairs. Deliah and Dominic burst into the room. Deliah took one look at her mother and ran up to her, folding her arms around her waist.

"Where have you been?" Deliah asked. "I've missed you. Have you heard from Damon?"

Charlotte stepped away from her daughter, removing her hands from her waist. She went back to unpacking as if no one was in the room. Deliah was shocked at her mother's nonchalance and started crying.

"Stop that," Charlotte scolded as she removed another necklace from a tiny blue bag, this one a delicate gold chain. "You're a princess. Pull yourself together. No, I haven't heard from Damon."

Ramos stepped up to Deliah and hugged her. Dominic was watching his mother sadly. Lana knew he was disappointed; she saw it in his face. Deliah ran out of the room. When no one said anything or made a move to follow, Dominic took off after his sister. Lana followed them out of the room, happy to be leaving her aunt's presence. When she reached the bottom of the staircase, she was surprised to see Terris and her parents. Her parents had held Dominic back but Deliah was nowhere to be seen.

"Is everything all right?" Jacqueline asked. "Deliah just ran past us. She seemed upset."

Lana shrugged. "She's mad that I met her family in Sumner. You think she'd be happy I'm all right."

Jacqueline sighed. "Let's find Deliah."

"She's probably on her way to Damon's bedroom," Dominic said. "She goes there a lot. I think she's been sleeping there."

They stepped out of the alcove, past the soldiers standing guard, into cooler air. They followed Dominic to Damon's room. Lana used the time to think about Madge, remembering how different she was than her sister. Madge and Henry had welcomed them. Even though Madge had seemed suspicious of Lana and Terris, she was at least welcoming.

When they were outside Damon's room, she thought about the last time she had seen her cousin. It was right before he jumped out of the window, hundreds of feet from the ground.

She had watched him step off the ledge, smiling the whole time.

Dominic opened the door to Deliah's sniffles. Damon's bedroom was cloaked in a velvety darkness. Deliah was curled up on her brother's bed, her body shaking with the force of her cries.

"Deliah." Dominic crawled into the bed with his sister. "It's all right."

Deliah turned toward her brother, crying into his shoulder. Jacqueline stepped up to the bed, and stroked Deliah's hair softly. Grayson stood at the door, watching the scene before him sadly.

Lana remained silent, unsure of what to say. She knew why her cousin was so upset. Her brother joined the rebels only to disappear, leaving his family to wonder if he was alive. Now her mother was ignoring her instead of comforting her. She would be a mess too.

"No," Deliah said, wiping her runny nose on the sleeve of her cloak. "It's not all right. I miss Damon. He's been gone for so long. No one's heard from him. Who knows if anyone is even looking for him."

"I'm sure he's fine," Dominic said soothingly.

"You don't know that!" Deliah sat up. "And what's wrong with Mom?"

"Deliah, your mother's under a lot of stress," Jacqueline said. "She had a long trip back."

"I know." Deliah erupted into violent hiccups. "But didn't she miss us?"

"Let's go to the Square." Jacqueline took Deliah's arm and helped her out of bed. "Fresh air will clear your head."

Lana had stopped listening. On the floor, at the foot of the bed, was a stack of yellowed paper. She saw the familiar handwriting and gasped.

Terris watched her. Lana looked around the room, making

sure he was the only one who had noticed before bending down, pretending she had dropped something. As she slowly inched closer to the papers, she knew without a doubt that Damon had made the drawings she found in Poklin's. Her mind raced.

"Lana?" Jacqueline called from the door, drawing her attention. "Did you hear us? We're going to the Square."

She looked up, trying to hide her surprise with a smile. Terris was still watching her, his lips pursed, and eyebrows raised. She wished she could talk to him alone and tell him what she had discovered.

"I heard," she lied, standing up.

Jacqueline didn't seem to think anything of her strange behavior and led Deliah and Dominic out of the bedroom. Terris crossed over to her, taking advantage of the empty room.

"Look at these," she said, bending down and picking up a few sheets.

"Damon's old lesson notes? What about them?"

She sighed, throwing her hands up in frustration. "Look at the handwriting. Does it look familiar?"

He studied the paper. A moment later, he looked at her, his face showing recognition and doubt at the same time. "You think he drew them?"

Grant walked into the room, watching them curiously. "What are you doing?"

She didn't want to tell him yet. Terris coughed, trying to buy time to think of an answer.

"I dropped my ring," she said. "We were only looking for it."

Grant motioned them out of the room, closing the door behind them. She twisted the ring around her finger. The green gems formed a leaf and sparkled when the light hit them just right. She learned Alderic had given the ring to her birth mother, Kalinia, many years ago. She liked wearing it as it reminded her of the mother she never knew.

"What kept you?" Grayson asked when they caught up to him.

"I lost my ring," she answered. She held up her hand, surprised at how easy it was becoming to lie. "Terris was helping me find it."

"Stay with your mother. I'll join you in the Square shortly."

She nodded, too consumed with her find. She wondered when Damon had made the sketches and for whom. Terris walked silently beside her.

As they walked over the drawbridge, she shivered. The brisk afternoon air chilled her. She wrapped her cloak tighter around herself and looked into the moat. A monogrose swam up to join another already at the surface, snapping its teeth wildly. The beasts resembled alligators, although they had pointy sharp spikes all over their bodies. She looked for the third but couldn't find it in the murky water.

While it had stopped raining, thick grey clouds covered the sky. She stepped over a puddle and carefully made her way to her mother, who was waiting for her at the end of the drawbridge. The fountain of Bridian stood tall in the middle of the courtyard, surrounded by houses and shops. A soldier followed them.

Gold, metallic sparks flew from the three circular tiers of the fountain in place of water and collected at the bottom in a pool of glittery sparkles. The fountain held the Orbs of Telorian, portals to other dimensions. Lana had been mesmerized when she first saw the Orbs. She had been surprised to learn the same portals were underneath the Great Sphinx of Giza in an underground chamber.

"Why do you think my mom is angry with you for meeting Aunt Madge and her family?" Dominic asked.

Jacqueline slowed her pace and joined them. Lana didn't know what to say because she was struggling with the answer to this question herself.

"I'm not sure. She wouldn't say. She just didn't sound happy about it."

"I've only met her once," Dominic said. "I don't think Mom has even mentioned her in the last few years. We always visit Aunt Lorna, never Aunt Madge."

"We didn't stay long," Lana said, turning back to the fountain.

By now, Terris and Deliah had fallen into step with them, curiosity getting the better of them. Jacqueline opened her mouth to say something, but Dominic beat her to the punch. "You met them too?" he asked Terris.

Jacqueline didn't wait for Terris to answer and said, "There's a reason for your mother's apprehension about Lana, or anyone else meeting her family in Sumner. If you promise to keep this to yourself, I'll tell you why."

Deliah and Dominic nodded in agreement. Lana sat down on the edge of the fountain.

"I've known your mother for many years. She grew up in a very wealthy and prominent family of Rochelle. Her father became king when she was a young girl. When he died, her younger sister, Madge, gained the throne."

Lana's heart skipped a beat. Maybe there was a way out of becoming Queen of Bridian after all. If Charlotte's younger sister had become queen, bypassing Charlotte, maybe there was someone else the throne of Bridian could pass to?

Jacqueline seemed to read her mind and said, "Things are different in Rochelle. The throne doesn't always pass to the eldest child. Your mom wasn't happy about that," she added, looking at Deliah and Dominic. "She always felt that it should have been her. She was blindsided."

"She's Queen of Bridian now," Lana said, not fully understanding the connection to her aunt's anger at meeting her family.

"It's only temporary. King Ramos is holding your place. When you take the throne, she'll no longer be queen."

Lana crossed her arms over her chest. Her uncle was only a substitute. It was tradition. The eldest child, male or female, gained the throne. She was Alderic's only child. The more she thought about it, the less she wanted to be Queen of Bridian. It wasn't for her. She would rather let someone who really wanted it hold the title.

"Why can't he just continue ruling Bridian?"

"The throne was never meant for him," Jacqueline answered sharply.

"But—"

"Lana," she interrupted, her forehead creased. "*You* are Alderic's only child and therefore the rightful ruler of Bridian."

Lana sighed. She knew there was no use arguing. She was clearly outnumbered, and it didn't matter that she was spiraling toward a future she didn't want.

"What were you saying about my mom?" Deliah frowned.

"She never understood her sister's decision," Jacqueline said carefully. "Madge gave up everything to marry Henry."

"That's why we're not allowed to visit them?" Dominic asked.

"Your mother is used to a certain lifestyle," Jacqueline said carefully. "She doesn't understand why her sister gave it all up. I imagine a part of her is also harboring a grudge. She's still angry. When Madge gave up the throne to marry Henry, their other sister Lorna became queen."

"Why was she so upset that we met them?" Lana asked.

"In a way, Madge is her secret." Jacqueline looked off into the distance. "She doesn't want people to know that her sister lives like a pauper instead of the royalty she could have been. Her family is one of the most influential families in Telorian. Image means everything to her."

Lana couldn't fathom the Queen's expectations. Madge had

seemed happy when they had met them. Even Karla, Nadia, and Ned looked content in their lives.

Lana was consumed in her thoughts when her vision blurred. She blinked, trying to clear her sight. Her hands began tingling again. She took a deep, calming breath. She heard her cousins talking next to her, but couldn't make out what was being said. It felt as if she were underwater. She closed her eyes and placed her hands on the fountain, trying to steady herself when she heard her mother.

"Lana? Are you—?"

She didn't finish the sentence. Lana looked up and saw Jacqueline in mid-stride, walking toward her. Her right leg was bent, her foot inches from the ground. Her left arm was straight in front of her, and her right arm was near her body, bent at an awkward angle.

She turned to her cousins. Deliah was standing near her brother with her mouth open as if she had been caught unaware mid-sentence. Both Dominic and Terris were watching her but there was something unnatural about the stillness. Grant and the soldier that had accompanied them reminded her of statues. Something was wrong.

She ran her eyes over the rest of the Square and found it silent and still. The fountain had stopped showering. The glittery water was suspended in the air. She stood up and slowly made her way to her mother. She touched her arm, hoping to wake her from her stupor. Jacqueline's skin was warm but stiff. She was staring ahead, her eyes trained on the fountain, exactly where Lana had been sitting.

"Mom? What's wrong?"

She didn't answer. Lana ran to Deliah and took her arm. When she too didn't move, she ran to Dominic, and Terris. The Square was eerily quiet. She went to Jacqueline again, gripping her arm tightly. She dug her nails into her skin, but even that didn't elicit a reaction.

Lana's throat closed as she stumbled backward, away from the scene before her. She tripped over her feet and fell, cutting her left hand on a jagged piece of rock. Bright red blood appeared but didn't trickle onto the skin. It appeared as if everything outside of her was suspended in time. She didn't think her life could get any more stressful, but it had, and she didn't know what to do.

4

THE FROSTED SQUARE

Lana ran toward the castle. She was surprised to see lights on in Poklin's and wondered who was in the shop when she heard the sound of running water. Blood trickled down her left hand. Voices made it to her ears again. It seemed as if a switch had been flipped, and time was ticking.

She turned around to see Jacqueline, Grant, Terris, and her cousins moving too. The water in the fountain was running down the tiered base—the sparkles reflecting in the sunlight through the clouds. Without thinking, she ran toward her mother, curling into her embrace.

"What's wrong?" Jacqueline asked, holding her tight. "How did you get over there?"

She wasn't sure how to answer. She didn't know what had happened. Was she losing her mind? Had time really stopped? If so, why hadn't it affected her?

"How did you get all the way over there?" Jacqueline asked again, pulling away from her so she could look into her eyes. "You were sitting at the fountain."

"I don't know," she said, trying to find the right words. "Everything was motionless. Including all of you. It was almost as if you were frozen—time had stopped. I don't know what happened."

"I don't remember that." Deliah crossed her arms over her chest. "I think that's something I would remember."

Grant stepped up behind her, his head tilted to the right as if he didn't quite believe what Lana was saying either. She didn't even believe what she had experienced. How was she supposed to explain it or convince anyone?

"I don't know how it happened. I was sitting at the fountain, and everyone just stopped moving. I even scratched you," she added, looking at her mother. "On your right arm."

Jacqueline's face paled when she saw the thin jagged marks on her skin.

"How is that possible?" Terris asked.

Jacqueline looked around nervously. "Let's get out of the open. We don't know if anyone saw anything."

"Oh, can we go to The Frosted Square?" Deliah clapped her hands together. "I want a marbellano." She didn't seem to be bothered by the strange course this day had taken or maybe she didn't believe her cousin.

"We can sit at our table," Dominic added. "They always save it for us. It's in a private room."

"Sure," Jacqueline replied without pause. She turned to the soldier who had accompanied them. "Can you please bring Grayson to The Frosted Square?"

The soldier nodded.

"Wait. I trust you'll keep this to yourself?" she added as an afterthought.

The soldier gave a non-committal jerk of his head but assented when Dominic and Deliah glared at him. He couldn't refuse the Prince and Princess.

Lana watched him take the path to the castle. A group of people, about her age, came out of a shop to their left. A girl was laughing so hard she had to lean against the boy next to her as if she would fall without his support. Lana envied them. She would give anything to switch places with them, to live a carefree life again.

"Let's go," Jacqueline said softly.

Deliah squealed in delight and Dominic ran ahead. Terris was quiet as he followed. Lana turned toward her mother and watched her shoot a worried look at Grant, her eyebrows were scrunched inward, and her lips were pressed in a tight frown. When she saw Lana watching, her lips turned up into a half-smile.

Suddenly, the girl from the shop stopped laughing. She elbowed the boy next to her. "Why'd you do that?" he asked angrily.

The girl stood taller, her shoulders pushed back and her chin up. The others in her group noticed the change in her demeanor and looked up to see Deliah and Dominic. When they bowed, her cousins kept walking, as if they hadn't even noticed. Once they had passed, the group began whispering excitedly to each other, until they saw Lana. She bit her lip and kept walking. It still surprised her how her cousins were so accustomed to the attention. No amount of people fazed them.

Deliah and Dominic walked up to the shop. A large window overlooked the fountain. A curtain of clear crystals reflected the light onto the Square. A teal sign hung over the wooden door. *The Frosted Square* was written in white block letters. White swirly lines curved around the shop name, outlining it. Dominic opened the door and ran inside, Deliah right behind him.

When Lana stepped into the shop, the smell of vanilla and sugar greeted her. Everything from the walls to the furniture was bright white. To their left was a tall white counter and a large display case filled with an assortment of cookies, cakes, and pies. A young woman, with short spiky hair, greeted them.

Deliah ran to the counter, unable to wait for the others.

Lana was more taken by the painting on the wall than the sweet treats. Thick white paint was spread about the canvas in random directions, the brushstrokes going every which way. It reminded her of frosting.

"I'll have a marbellano," Deliah said happily.

"How lovely to see you," a familiar voice said, entering the room from the backdoor.

An older woman with tightly curled hair, who looked like the owner of the shop, stepped into the room. She was wearing a lavender dress and a matching silk scarf was tied around her neck. She was even wearing lavender frosted lipstick.

"Oh," the woman squealed excitedly when she saw Lana. "I was hoping I would see you again."

As the door swung shut, the woman walked to the counter, joining the younger woman. Lana searched her mind. She recognized the voice, but couldn't place her and it was driving her crazy.

"Thank you, Samoa," Jacqueline said, peering out of the window. "Grayson will be joining us shortly. Is there someplace private we can sit?"

The woman pointed to the backdoor. At the mention of her name, the pieces clicked, and Lana remembered meeting her. She had been wearing a bright orange dress at her uncle's birthday party, right before Alderic and Damon crashed the festivities.

Deliah led the way to the backdoor.

"I'll take one too," Dominic called.

"Would you like anything?" Jacqueline asked Lana and Terris.

Samoa set a silver tray on the counter. "I'll bring some extras for everyone."

The shop door opened, and Grayson hurried in. His breathing was heavy, as if he had been running. When he saw Jacqueline, he rushed to her.

"Is everything all right?" he asked as a woman and a young boy walked in, stepping around Grayson and Jacqueline awkwardly. "Lana, are you all right?"

She nodded.

"We can talk in private," Jacqueline said, eyeing the newcomers suspiciously.

Lana and Terris followed her parents to the backdoor. When they entered the hallway she heard Deliah and Dominic. Their voices were raised. When she caught her friend's eye they burst into laughter at her cousins' antics. They walked through the clean white hallway to a door, following the sound of their voices.

Her cousins were at a large table. Dominic sat on a chair and Deliah stood behind him, sulking. Her hands were crossed over her chest and her eyes were narrowed at the back of her brother's head.

"What's the problem?" Grayson asked.

"This is the chair I always sit in," Deliah pouted, her hands gripping her brother's chair. "He won't move."

Terris walked to the table and sat next to Dominic. He pulled out the chair to his left and looked at Deliah.

"This chair is even better," he said. "Look, it's directly underneath the light and you can see into the hallway."

Deliah glared at her brother, willing him to vacate the chair. When that didn't work, she sighed loudly and sat in the offered chair next to Terris. Everyone else seated themselves without any further drama.

Lana turned to her cousin. "You couldn't give her the chair?"

Dominic's eyes lit up. "Nope, this is more fun."

Grant remained near the door to allow them privacy and prevent anyone else from entering. Lana looked at her father, hoping he would have an explanation for the incident in the Square.

"So, what happened?" he asked.

When no one answered, she looked at her mother, waiting for her to explain, but she remained silent. In the time it took her to gather her thoughts, Samoa waltzed in. She stepped between Dominic and Lana's chairs, placing napkins and a silver tray filled with large cookies topped with what looked like powdered sugar on the table.

"We're all so glad that you're back," Samoa said, looking at Lana.

Dominic reached for the cookies. He slid one to Lana on a pale yellow napkin.

"Dom," Deliah called. "What about us," she asked, pointing to herself and Terris. "We want one too."

Dominic rolled his eyes. He slid the tray toward his sister and sat back down.

"How do you like it here?" Samoa asked, still looking at Lana. "It must be quite different from where you grew up."

"Everything's kind of a blur," Lana said, pulling her napkin closer. "I'm still adjusting."

"Well, everyone's happy you're back." When she saw Lana playing with the napkin she said, "These are our specialty. It's a marbellano. I make them fresh every day. Every week I send an order to Princess Deliah. I know she likes them."

"Oh, I do," Deliah said, white sugar coating her lips.

"Has there been any word on Alderic?" Samoa asked, looking at Jacqueline and Grayson. "Or the rest of them? It doesn't feel right that Poklin's is closed."

"We haven't heard anything," Grayson said, setting his hands on the table.

Samoa looked at Lana, her eyes searching deep within hers. Lana picked up the marbellano, hoping Samoa would leave so she could tell her father what happened. As she bit into the cookie, she was surprised when the sweetest red jam spilled out.

"How do you like it?" Samoa asked, her hands clasped in front of her and bouncing on her toes.

Lana set the cookie down on her napkin. While it was delicious, it was too sweet for her.

"It's very good."

Samoa smiled widely. "That's marbellano jam. You didn't have marbellano trees where you grew up?"

Lana shook her head. She could add marbellano trees to her growing list of subtle differences between Bridian and Mt. Sinclair that also included magic, Choclochino's, Shadow Splinters, fairies, and mermaids.

"They're like strawberries," Grayson added. "Only sweeter."

"Strawberries?" Deliah asked, looking up from her cookie.

"Can we have a moment Samoa?" Jacqueline asked, her tone sharp.

Samoa nodded. "I'll pack a box to go for Princess Deliah."

"Thanks!" Deliah said with a charming smile, reaching for another.

The entire exchange overwhelmed Lana. She was in tears by the end of it. Everything in her life had changed so much already and the only thing that was constant was change itself. She wanted strawberry jam, not marbellano jam. She didn't know why she was crying, but it felt good to release the pent-up anger and confusion—the fear and the frustration.

Dominic handed her another napkin. "What's wrong with you?"

"Lana," Grayson said. "What happened?"

She wiped the tears from her eyes. Jacqueline knelt in front of her, squeezing her hand.

"We were in the Square," she began.

She stopped to take a deep, calming breath. Out of the corner of her eyes, she saw Dominic watching her, his eyes wide. He couldn't understand why she had been crying. Deliah was still focused on her cookie.

She turned back to her father. "My hands began tingling but I ignored it. But then everyone just froze. It was like suspended animation. Time stopped for everyone but me."

Her parents looked at each other, appraising the situation and silently conferring. A tear slid down her cheek but she quickly wiped it away.

"I don't know how it happened," she continued. "Or even if it really happened. Maybe I imagined it."

"You didn't imagine it." Jacqueline sighed. "One minute you were sitting on the fountain ledge and the next you were across the Square."

Grayson looked around the room. "We knew this would happen." When Jacqueline narrowed her eyes, he continued. "Well, we knew the magic would manifest. We were waiting to see how it would develop."

"She stopped time, Grayson," Jacqueline said, still squeezing Lana's hand. "That isn't normal magic."

"Right," Grayson said slowly, searching for the right words. "When you found the Crystal, you held it?"

Lana nodded. She didn't know what holding the Crystal had to do with anything. Terris inhaled deeply, his eyes wide.

"I don't get it. What does the Crystal have to do with time stopping?"

"When you touched it, you siphoned some of the magic," he said. "That's my best guess."

"Have you noticed anything else?" Jacqueline asked. "Anything else strange?"

Lana's stomach knotted. She wished her grandfather hadn't left her the clues to find the Crystal. She wished she hadn't pieced the mystery together. She wished she hadn't found it.

"That was weeks ago," she said a moment later, still fixated on the revelation about the Crystal. "Why is it happening now?"

"It's probably been building up," Grayson answered. "Along with the magic around us."

"Has anything else happened?" Jacqueline repeated. "Anything?"

She shook her head. "No, nothing like that. I've been having a lot of headaches and tingling in my hands but nothing as strange as this."

A knock on the door interrupted them. Before anyone could answer, the door reopened, and Samoa walked in holding a large white box, tied with a white bow. She set it on the table in front of Deliah.

"Excuse the interruption," she said with a wide grin on her face. "I didn't want you to leave without your treats."

Grayson stood. "Thank you, Samoa. We better get back."

"Be careful," Samoa said. "Last week someone broke into Poklin's."

Grayson stopped walking. "That's odd, the store's empty."

Lana gasped. Had rebels broken into Poklin's?

Samoa changed the subject, explaining the newest creation coming to the shop as they walked down the hall into the main storefront.

Terris made his way to Lana when everyone's attention was focused on Samoa's treat. "Do you think they were looking for the papers?"

She nodded. She didn't want her parents to hear their conversation. A few customers stood near the display case, eagerly selecting their orders. A heavy silence fell upon the room when they noticed Deliah and Dominic. But the crowd ran abuzz again when their gaze fell on Lana.

"Is that her?" a young boy asked.

"It has to be," another said. "She's with Prince Dominic and Princess Deliah."

The customers bowed. Deliah and Dominic continued on

their way. Samoa walked them to the door, still talking to Jacqueline and Grayson. Lana's brain was spinning.

"It was lovely to see you again," Samoa said to Lana, bowing. "Come back soon."

"The marbellano was delicious. Thank you."

She turned to exit the shop and saw that Deliah and Dominic were already gone. They were talking happily, oblivious to Samoa's comment about Poklin's. Terris walked beside her, lost in thought.

Grayson placed his hand on her shoulder. "We'll figure this out. Don't worry."

She wondered how she was supposed to not worry. All she could think about was making time stop again. What if next time it didn't restart? She didn't know how she had made it happen in the first place. She couldn't imagine being alone forever with everyone else in a state of perpetual suspension.

"Lana?" Grayson asked, breaking her from her thoughts. "Are you listening?"

She looked up. They were near the fountain, in the same place where it had happened. Her parents were both looking at her. They had stopped walking. Dominic had his arms over his chest and Deliah was tapping her foot dramatically.

"I'm sorry. I wasn't listening,"

"You don't remember what you were doing when it happened?" Grayson asked. "Or what you were thinking?"

She shook her head. "Mom was talking. She was telling us about Queen Charlotte's family, and then it happened."

He nodded and then led them to the drawbridge. No one uttered a single word. Lana's mind raced—she wanted answers.

When they passed the alley leading to the back entrance of Poklin's, she saw the door open slowly. Her heart beat rapidly within her chest as someone in a long dark robe closed the door. The cloaked figure looked up at her. Her breath caught in her throat. She wondered if it was a rebel when the figure began running toward them.

5

BROTHERS REUNITED

Grant sprang in front of Lana. She was so startled she bumped into Jacqueline who was holding the box from The Frosted Square. Deliah and Dominic were walking ahead of her, oblivious to the altercation behind them. Deliah was talking loudly, her hands gesturing wildly. Lana couldn't understand what she was saying, she was too focused on the man running toward them from Poklin's. Was it a rebel? Alderic? Contlay? Damon?

She was relieved when the mysterious figure finally came within her line of sight.

"Can you help me?" the stranger said.

Her father grasped Lana's hands, shielding her in case the man attacked.

Grant took the lead, eyeing the man cautiously. "What are you doing here? The shop is closed."

"I'm trying to close the door. I can't get it to lock, and I have to return the keys to King Ramos." The man held his hand out to Grant, showing him a long, thin silver key. "I see you're a soldier for Bridian," he continued. "I have somewhere to be and just need a little help."

"I'll help him," Grant said, looking at Grayson. "You go on ahead."

Grayson nodded and gestured for Lana to join him, but she didn't move. She wanted to go inside to see if any other clues had been left behind, something that would tell her the significance of the drawings. Since Samoa mentioned the store had been broken into last week, she was even more curious.

"Why don't we all help," Lana said, her voice cracking. "It's right there. I could use the extra walk after the marbellano."

"Oh, maybe there's leftover candy." Deliah clapped her hands together excitedly.

"Just what you need, Deliah." Dominic laughed.

The man frowned. Recognition dawned on his face and he bowed.

"I hate to be the one to have to tell you this. The shop's empty."

Deliah lowered her head. Lana watched the man closely. Why did he have keys to Poklin's?

"I'm sorry," he said, looking at Grant. "I didn't realize you were with the Prince and Princess. I can find someone else to help."

The man was tall, taller than her father and Grant. He had broad shoulders and his dark skin was flawless.

"We can help," Lana said, turning to him. "Right? It should only take a minute."

Grayson narrowed his eyes. "What's gotten into you?"

"It's nice to be outside. It'll help take my mind off everything."

"I don't know," Jacqueline said.

Lana knew Jacqueline was worried about her. She was worried, so her mother had to be—and she could use that to her advantage.

"If the shop's empty, what's the point?" Deliah sighed.

She looked at her cousin, silently urging her to be quiet.

Dominic sensed that she was up to something and elbowed his sister.

"You could use the walk too, Del."

Grayson and Jacqueline were clearly confused with her insistence but relented. The man led them to the backdoor of the shop. The door was ajar, and the alley was empty.

"Let's look inside." Lana turned to Deliah. "You never know, you might find some leftover candy after all."

Deliah ran to the front of the group, but Grayson held his arm out before she could run up the stairs.

"Not so fast," he said, stepping in front of her. "I'll go first."

He walked up the stairs and pushed the door open. The tiny bell above the doorframe rang. As Grayson made his way inside the dark shop, Terris stepped next to her.

"Do you think something may have been left behind?"

Lana nodded. When her father motioned that it was safe to go inside, she ran in. As the man had said, the shop was bare. She looked around the store, trying to see in the dim light. Everything had been emptied, even the shelves. She was standing in an unfurnished room, save for the bar at the front of the shop. When Ramos said he was going to strip the store, he had really meant it.

She ran her hand along the smooth surface of the bar top. Faint light leaked through the dusty windows, still advertising Poklin's Variety Store, the name scribbled backward in a thin layer of dust. She remembered the first time she had visited the shop. She had snuck out of the castle with Kiernan. Lana saw Poklin's now as she had for the first time. For a moment, brightly colored candy was neatly displayed on shelves. Children played with toys while adults sipped drinks at the bar.

She had also met Alexander that day. She had been sitting at the bar, talking to Poklin when Alexander recognized her, lifted her off the stool, and brought her back to the castle. She shuddered as she thought of the last time she had seen him. He had been coming out of the deep sleep the rebels had put him under. She heard their shovels hitting the ground as they excavated him from his grave. She hoped Ramos would rescue him soon.

Lana watched her parents. They were talking softly, every so often glancing at her. She turned to Terris.

"I want to check the back room. Maybe someone left something there."

He nodded. Her cousins were near the bar, arguing over the best candy Poklin had sold. As they made their way to the room, she hoped that she would find something to help her unravel the mystery. Perhaps her life would go back to normal if she found the Crystal.

Her spirits fell when she saw the door was already open. She stepped into yet another empty room. Even the furniture had been removed. She heard footsteps behind her and turned around.

"This would be my office," the man said, stepping past Lana. "I'd keep the same layout."

"Are you going to rent the shop?" Dominic asked, joining them.

"I'm considering it. Did you come here often?"

"Whenever Dad would let us," Deliah said.

"What will you sell?" Terris asked.

"Candy, toys, everything Poklin sold. But I want to reopen the store under a new name. My name's Gareth," he added with a courtly bow.

She turned to Terris, disappointed that they hadn't found anything. His lips curled into a slight frown, and she knew he was just as disappointed as she was. They followed Gareth to the back door again.

"The door won't lock. The key won't turn."

Grant gestured for everyone to go outside. "Let's see what I can do." He closed the door and fumbled with the key. A moment later, he turned around. "You have to turn the key to the left first. You may want to have the locks changed."

"Ah, thank you," Gareth said, catching the key Grant tossed at him. "I apologize for keeping you."

Deliah and Dominic renewed their stroll to the castle. Lana followed, Terris by her side. Her parents and Grant were behind them, speaking to Gareth. Jacqueline was so close to Lana she stepped on her feet more than once.

When they rounded the corner, she saw a small garden filled with vegetables. Two large stone benches were on either side of the plot. It was tucked away in between shops, effectively concealing it. She would have to come back and visit the peaceful garden another time.

When they were inside the castle, Deliah took the box from The Frosted Square from Jacqueline.

"Where are you going with those?" Dominic called.

When Deliah didn't answer, he ran after her. Lana watched him chase his sister down and try to take the box out of her hands. She listened to their laughter and a pit formed in her stomach.

"Lana, are you listening?" Jacqueline asked.

She turned to her parents. They were both watching her, Jacqueline's forehead furrowed.

"I'm sorry," she said sheepishly.

"I'm going to stay with you tonight," she said. "In case something else happens."

Lana nodded. Although she hoped that things would go back to some semblance of normal, she couldn't be sure, and it would be nice to have her mother with her.

"Do you think anyone can help me? Make this stop?"

"I'm going to talk with King Ramos," Grayson said. "We'll figure this out. Don't worry."

She didn't know what to say. Her eyes were heavy and all she wanted to do was lay down for a moment.

"I'm going to go to my room," she said. "Finish my homework."

Jacqueline bit her lip as if she was fighting back the urge to say something. Grayson narrowed his eyes at her, clearly concerned.

"I'll be up in a bit," Jacqueline finally said.

Lana looked at Terris. She gestured for him to walk with her. Grant followed a few feet behind them.

"Are you thinking the same thing?" she whispered. "The break-in is tied to the papers?"

"Maybe? It could just be random."

She stopped walking and turned to him, narrowing her eyes.

"I know, I know," he said, a smile spreading across his face. "You think they're the key to the Crystal. Even if you find it again, your life won't magically go back to how it was in Mt. Sinclair. It won't solve everything."

Lana raised her eyebrows at her friend. "If you find your parents, it won't solve everything."

His face fell and she knew she had taken it too far. She needed to be supportive and at this point, she was being anything but.

"I'm sorry."

He nodded. "No, you're right."

The air around them was tense. The events in the Square had her rattled. She was still trying to come to terms with what had happened, and how drastically her life had changed in just a short amount of time. Taking it out on her friend wasn't the best idea but she didn't know how to fix it.

As soon as she stepped inside her bedroom, she removed the papers from the trunk at the foot of her bed and sat on the floor. Terris sat next to her. She spread the drawings on her bent knees, studying them for anything that she may have missed.

"What if it happens again?" Lana asked.

Terris looked up at her. Her stomach fell, making her nauseous. She closed her eyes, reliving the moment time had stopped. There had to be a trigger. She just had to figure it out.

"I'm scared," she added.

"It didn't last long, right?" he said, offering her a weak smile. "At least you know if it happens again it isn't permanent."

They sat in silence a moment longer. She wondered if he really believed that, or was only telling her what he thought she wanted to hear. Terris reached for the papers.

"Maybe it's someplace in Medora?" he said. "You know, somewhere in the caves, where he met the Revatto?"

Lana couldn't think straight. Too many thoughts were swimming in her head, vying for space. She folded the papers and put them back in her cloak.

"I think I want to lay down," she said, the events of the day finally overtaking her. "I just want to be alone."

"I should go anyway." Terris stood. "I have to work soon." He turned back when he reached the door. "Everything will be okay."

Lana hoped he was right. She kicked off her shoes, and collapsed on the bed. She knew she should work on her homework but wasn't in the mood. Her life was spiraling out of control. What did homework matter?

She pulled her blue daisy quilt up to her chin and closed her eyes. When she reopened them, she was no longer in her bedroom. In fact, she wasn't even in the castle. She had been transported to a dark forest, surrounded by lots of green, leafy trees. The air was hot and humid, and the ground was covered in thick undergrowth. Everything was silent.

She began running, hoping to find a way back to the castle. She didn't remember leaving and wondered where she was and how long she'd been gone. She raced through a patch of trees in front of her, pushing her way through branches that scratched her skin. She heard something behind her but didn't look back. Beads of sweat trickled down her face and her lungs screamed for air.

All of the sudden, bright light filled her vision. It was as if someone had flipped a switch, illuminating a very dark room. She was so taken aback at the scene, she stopped running, shielding her eyes from the intense light. Her heart pounded within her chest, trying to escape. She stumbled, lost her balance, and fell to the ground.

Before she had a chance to stand she heard rustling and looked at the sky. She saw hundreds of sheets of paper fall all around her. With shaking hands, she reached for one of the crisp white papers but it was blank. They all were.

As quickly as it had begun, the torrent of papers stopped. She watched the last sheet sink to the ground, inches from her. She stood up, jumping when she heard the sound of glass breaking.

All around her, balls of glass were falling, shattering into a million little pieces when they hit the ground. She stood rooted, unsure where to go. She threw her arms over her head, but the balls seemed to be repelled by her. Not a single one hit her.

Lana began running again. She found herself in a large, open field. A dark figure was in the distance. She tried to stop running, but her legs continued to move, as if independent from her. A pale hand emerged from the cloak, reaching for her.

"Lana."

The cloaked figure was calling her name, still reaching toward her. She thought she heard her name again and her body trembled.

"Wake up, Lana."

She was pulled away from the forest, away from the eerie figure and the pale hand. She opened her eyes and saw Jacqueline next to her. She was in her pajamas and her hair was in a messy ponytail. She had dark circles underneath her eyes.

"You must have been having a nightmare. You were screaming."

Lana tried to steady her breathing. Bright sunshine poured in from the window.

"What time is it?"

Jacqueline turned toward the clock. "Eight in the morning. You slept straight through dinner last night. You looked so peaceful I didn't want to wake you."

She sat up. "I guess I was tired."

Jacqueline took her hand and squeezed it. "I'm going to get dressed. I'll come back and we can go down to the dining hall for breakfast together."

After she left, Lana got out of bed and showered. She dressed in a pair of dark blue jeans and a Mt. Sinclair T-shirt. Even though her clothes made her stand out, they were comfortable. They reminded her of a simpler time.

She put her hair in a bun and sat down on the bed to wait for her mother. She thought of her dream and shivered. It had felt so real.

A few minutes later, Jacqueline joined her. She looked refreshed. Her hair was curled, and her blue eyes were lined with mascara.

"So, your big day is only a few weeks away," she said with a little too much excitement.

Lana didn't know what she was talking about. When she didn't say anything her mother sighed.

"Did you forget your birthday?"

"Oh, I guess I did," she said, tracing the outline of the daisies on her quilt. "Probably because there's nothing to celebrate."

Jacqueline frowned. "There's always something to celebrate. You're going to be sixteen."

"Let's skip it this year. It's just another day to get through."

Lana stood up, reached for her cloak, and put it on. Jacqueline saw her discarded crown on the trunk and picked it up. She walked to Lana and placed it on her head carefully.

"You look beautiful."

She rolled her eyes. "Thanks, Mom."

Her stomach rumbled as they made their way to the dining hall. Grant followed quietly. She looked at the portraits on the wall as they walked, smiling when they reached a woman wearing an ugly blue dress that reminded her of her Aunt Charlotte.

She looked over the railing at the crowd of people at the dining hall entrance and spotted Kiernan among them. He walked to the bottom of the staircase, waiting for her. Lana climbed down the stairs gingerly, hoping she wouldn't trip.

"Hi," he said, smiling widely at her.

Lana smiled back. She couldn't help it. Something about him made her giddy. She looked at her mother, silently urging her to leave, but she didn't get the message.

"Good morning, Kiernan."

She nudged her mom. "I'll meet you inside."

"Don't be too long," she said, turning on her heels and walking into the dining hall.

Kiernan looked to the ground. She cleared her throat, thinking of something to start the conversation.

"Are you ready for class today?"

Once the words escaped her lips she immediately regretted them. She imagined pulling them back into her mouth, wishing she had said something else, something clever. Kiernan furrowed his brow, stepping closer to her.

"What did you say? I didn't hear you."

Lana narrowed her eyes. She had said the words loud enough for Kiernan to hear but he seemed genuinely confused, as if he had already forgotten what she had said. She had imagined the words coming back to her. Could that have actually happened? Could she control what people heard now? Or was it a coincidence?

In her confusion, she forgot all about sounding smart. "Nothing. How are you?"

"Tired," he answered. "I've been working with my father lately."

"Hey, Kiernan," Dominic said, pushing his way between them. "I thought you were going to play Parsneakity last night? We were waiting for you."

Kiernan shuffled on his feet. "I had to finish my homework."

Dominic took over the conversation, filling them in on their game. She looked up at Kiernan and saw that he was still watching her. Deliah came up behind them. Lana knew she wouldn't get a chance to talk to him alone now.

"I'm going to sit down," she said.

"I'll walk you to lessons," Kiernan called after her.

She nodded and Deliah grabbed her arm, leading her into the dining hall. As she took a sip of her dandelion tea, two men walked into the room with Ramos. Her father gasped.

"Grayson," one of the men called, holding his arms out as if waiting to embrace him.

"Elijah? Calum?" Grayson said.

Lana wondered who the men were and was shocked when her father ran to them. They hugged.

She turned to Jacqueline. "Who are they?"

"His brothers."

Lana instantly felt nauseous. She grew up believing Jacqueline and Grayson had no other family. Since returning to Bridian, she hadn't really given it much thought. The fact that her father had brothers that he hadn't seen in fifteen years made her sick.

"Do you also have brothers and sisters?" she asked.

Jacqueline nodded. "They live in Rochelle. Maybe when everything calms down, we can visit them."

Lana turned back to her father and saw he was making his way toward them, his brothers right behind him. She studied them. They looked like her father. They had the same brown eyes and stocky build.

"This is Lana," Grayson introduced her.

She smiled. "Nice to meet you."

"These are my brothers. Calum," he pointed to the shorter man on his right, "and Elijah," he said, gesturing to the man to his left.

Calum put his arm around Grayson. "We've missed you, little brother."

Jacqueline stood from her chair and walked to Elijah. She hugged him tightly and proceeded to hug Calum too. Two chairs were brought to the table. Ramos watched the reunion, a small smile on his lips. He sensed Lana's gaze and turned to Charlotte.

Shortly after, breakfast was served. The room filled with happy conversation and food. Lana loaded her plate with eggs and bacon. She was more of a listener today and contributed little to the talk but something Calum said struck her.

"He's been seen. In Medora."

Grayson and Jacqueline exchanged a knowing look. Calum was referring to Alderic. He wouldn't be in Medora, let alone be discovered, unless he had good reason. The demons were almost released there fifteen years ago. Deep down Lana knew Contlay never had the Crystal. It was in Medora with Alderic the entire time.

6

———

LESSONS

When she realized Lana had been listening to their conversation, Jacqueline quickly changed the subject. Lana tapped her fork against her plate in between sips of tea. Her stomach churned. She wasn't sure if it was the news of Alderic or the anticipation of walking to class with Kiernan.

When it was time to leave for class, she flew out of her chair. She heard Deliah and Dominic behind her and sighed. So much for avoiding their questions.

"What are you waiting for?" Deliah called over her shoulder as she passed.

"Nothing. I'll be up in a minute."

A moment later, Kiernan walked out with Terris. They were laughing. She noticed that they had been spending more time together. They usually sat near each other at meals when Terris wasn't working.

"How are you feeling?" Terris asked.

Lana discreetly shook her head, hoping Kiernan wouldn't notice. She didn't want to talk about it around him. Even though she felt better physically, the news of Alderic being seen in Medora unnerved her. She wanted to tell her friend what she learned, but not in front of Kiernan.

"Good," she answered. "We can talk later."

Terris raised his eyebrow but dropped the subject. Kiernan shifted his weight from side to side as an awkward silence fell upon them. To add to the discomfort, Grant was standing near the door, watching their exchange.

Terris cleared his throat. "I left something in my room. I'll meet you there."

Lana watched him walk away and wondered if he was just making an excuse to slide out of an uneasy situation.

"Do you have everything?" Kiernan asked.

She nodded. "Grant has my books."

At the mention of his name, Grant interrupted them. "You better hurry. Lessons start in a few minutes."

She narrowed her eyes at him. He smirked. It felt like she had another father watching over her. Kiernan chuckled and they made their way to the library. It was embarrassing to have an audience. Her thoughts shifted to her sixteenth birthday. She had always imagined Ava and Trevor with her. But the memory of the disaster that was her uncle's birthday made her shiver.

"I never did thank you," she whispered, hoping Grant wouldn't hear.

His brow furrowed. "For what?"

"For diverting attention from me," she answered. "From Alderic."

He shrugged. "Anyone would have done it."

Lana tried to think of something else to say, but Grant's presence made her too nervous. She breathed in the smell of the books as they entered the library. She loved the room. It was welcoming, warm. In Mt. Sinclair she had never gone to the public library, or even the school library. Now she realized what she had been missing, there was a certain peace to be found amongst the old leather-bound tomes.

She followed Kiernan to the stairs and they made their way to the second floor where lessons were held. Carter called out to Kiernan, waving him over.

Kiernan acknowledged him but turned back to Lana. "Do you want to eat lunch together?"

Her voice cracked in response. "Sure."

Kiernan made his way to Carter. Lana sat and Grant placed her books in front of her. At the same time, Nick walked into the room with his mother. Mrs. Jacobs waved at her before giving her son a big hug. Nick locked eyes with her and she gestured to one of the empty chairs close to her own, trying to be welcoming. Instead, he rolled his eyes and went to sit with Maris who was also waving him over.

Lana looked around the room, surprised to see the younger children had joined them for the day. Every child in the castle had lessons together, however the younger children didn't join them every day. She was still trying to figure out the schedule. Maris stood up to introduce Nick to the class.

After introductions, Maris asked everyone to turn in their papers. Dominic groaned loudly.

Lana raised her hand. "I haven't finished mine yet."

"Same," Randy added, placing his elbows on the table and cradling his head in his hands.

Mrs. DeGette was in the process of gathering the younger children to take them downstairs when Orin began crying. He threw himself to the ground. This set off a chain reaction as the boys next to him, Lowell and Marcus, began crying too.

Ivan shook his head. "Really, I don't see why we have to have class with them."

"Seriously." Nick stood up. "Why am I here?"

Mrs. DeGette stepped forward, holding her hands out as

Maris helped Orin up. "Quiet. Everyone take three deep breaths."

Lana inhaled deeply, following Mrs. DeGette's lead. Around her, pandemonium continued to reign supreme. Ivan was laughing. Deliah and Dominic were getting on each other's nerves, bickering loudly. Kiernan was joking around with Marnie. The only quiet ones were Terris and herself. Her friend was huddled over his paper, drawing something.

"Everyone up," Maris sighed. "Grant, we're going outside. Everyone needs to reconnect."

Grant nodded. His eyes wide from the chaos that had erupted around him. Lana stood, wondering what *reconnect* meant. She looked out the window and saw bright sunshine, which cheered her spirits. She liked spending time outdoors and was looking forward to the break.

Maris led them into the hallway. Mrs. DeGette wrangled the smaller children, while Maris led everyone else down the stairs to the first floor. Lana started to make her way to her cousins but then thought better of it when she saw that they were both glaring at each other. She didn't want to make it worse.

Maris led them outside, near the stables, into a large field. Across the field, the forest sat. Lana wondered what other mysteries it held. When everyone began removing their shoes without any directions from the instructor, she was puzzled. She looked at Nick, the only other person who hadn't grown up in Bridian, and saw he was just as confused as she was.

When Maris saw Lana and Nick just standing there, watching everyone else, she walked over to them. "Take your shoes off."

"Why?" Lana asked.

"Can this place get any weirder?" Nick muttered under his breath.

Maris cocked her head. "You didn't reconnect in Mt. Sinclair?"

"To what?" Lana asked.

Maris stepped out of her shoes and removed her socks. When her bare feet were on the ground, she closed her eyes and inhaled deeply.

"Every now and again, we need to reconnect with our home."

"Deliah, move over," Dominic demanded, pushing his sister away.

Deliah fell to the ground. She grunted and stood up, moving away from her brother.

"Quiet," Mrs. DeGette said, holding her hands up. "Everyone take a few minutes to ground yourself."

Lana did as she was told. She removed her sneakers and socks. The grass tickled her feet. It felt strange to be standing barefoot, and eyes closed, in the field with her classmates. She made it ten seconds before opening them again. Nick was sitting on the ground, twirling a blade of grass in his hands, but everyone else was religiously following instructions. Grant noticed her eyes were open and gestured for her to shut them.

She sighed loudly but decided to *reconnect*. The sunshine warmed her. Birds were chirping and a soft breeze blew around them. She was beginning to feel relaxed, rejuvenated even, when Dominic interrupted the silence.

"You're too close to me Deliah."

"Well, it worked for a moment," Maris said to Mrs. DeGette. "All right, does everyone feel a little calmer now?"

"No." Dominic took a wide step to his left, away from his sister. "I couldn't concentrate with her in my space."

Carter shrugged. "I feel better."

"Me too," Marnie added.

Lana sat on the grass and put her socks back on. "What was the point of that?"

"Our planet's energy flows through our bare feet and rebalances us—improves our mood, gives us energy," Maris said, gesturing around them.

Nick stood up and walked away from the group. "I'm done."

Grant reached out, as if he were going to stop him, when Mrs. DeGette said, "Nick, come sit with me."

He grudgingly made his way to her and sat on the grass again. Lana laced her sneakers and stood. The mood had definitely improved—everyone was talking happily. She watched Terris stumble forward, falling back to the ground. Kiernan helped him stand and they laughed.

"Who wants to play a quick game?" Maris asked. When everyone but Lana raised their hands, she added. "Good, after that, it's back to lessons. We have a lot to cover today."

Lana hoped the game wasn't Parsneakity. Maris asked Carter and Randy to help her set up and they went off toward a large shed. Deliah clapped her hands excitedly.

Grant stepped closer to Lana, seeming to remember the last game of Parsneakity, when she had left the castle with Kiernan. A moment later, Maris, Carter, and Randy rejoined them. They were each carrying an orange hoop.

Carter threw his hoop to Dominic, who caught it effortlessly. He twirled it around his finger.

Deliah held her arms out. "Throw it to me."

Dominic tossed the hoop in her direction, but he threw it too high. She jumped for it, but it flew high above her outstretched arms. Ivan caught it.

"That wasn't nice, Dom!" Deliah shrieked.

Ivan tossed the hoop back at Deliah, but she hadn't been paying attention and it hit her in the head. She stumbled, making Dominic and Ivan laugh.

"What happened?" Maris asked, narrowing her eyes.

"He did that on purpose." Deliah stomped her foot. "Ivan threw it at my head."

"I didn't mean for it to hit her," he said, holding his hands out in front of him.

Maris began lecturing Ivan about responsibility. Dominic grinned, trying to suppress his laughter. Lana looked for Kiernan, shielding her eyes from the bright sunshine. When she saw him across the field talking to Marnie, her stomach fell.

"How do you play?" she asked, turning to Terris before jealousy overtook her.

"You have to collect the most hoops," he said, watching Maris and Ivan's exchange. "You catch them."

Maris turned away from Ivan. "One quick game."

While everyone spread out Kiernan walked over to her, waving to Marnie as he left. Kiernan put his hands behind his back and looked around at everyone. "Do you know how to play?"

"Terris already explained the game. Just catch the hoops right?"

Before he could answer, Maris threw the large hoop in the air. Everyone scrambled for it as it rose higher and higher. Lana had been expecting it to fall on the ground and was surprised when it didn't. A moment later, two more hoops joined the first.

Orin ran in front of her, tripping over the same rut Terris had fallen over. Lana bent down to help him, and Marnie ran into her. She fell next to Orin and he started laughing. Marnie took off, without an apology.

Lana stood up. She brushed the dirt from her clothes. Everyone screamed excitedly. She looked up and saw the hoops falling. Dominic ran to her, pushing her out of the way and she fell down again. Her cousin jumped over her, catching a hoop, almost pulling it from the air.

"I got one!" he called excitedly before looking down at Lana. "You're never going to catch anything down there."

Before she could answer, Deliah joined them, her arms

crossed over her chest. "You pushed her, Dom. That wasn't nice."

"It's fine. I'm done playing anyway," Lana said.

She hobbled over to Maris and Mrs. DeGette. Nick had been sitting on the grass near them, not interested in participating. She heard Carter yell that he caught a hoop. She looked up, hoping the game was almost over. A smaller hoop was still floating in the air. A crowd gathered beneath it. Deliah and Ivan were jumping, their arms reaching for the elusive hoop.

"How's it floating?" she asked.

"That would be me," Mrs. DeGette said. "You gave up quickly."

"I'd rather watch."

"Sometimes it's good to try new things," Mrs. DeGette said. "If you're confused, ask for help rather than give up. A little extra advice that you can apply to your overdue paper."

Kiernan caught her eye. She smiled at him, which he took as an invitation to join her on the grass.

"Are you okay?" he asked. She only nodded in response.

The remaining hoop made its way to the ground, and she pointed at where the others were gathered. Deliah reached for the hoop but Dominic pushed her out of the way. She fell backward on Terris. As Terris was helping her stand, Ivan pushed him out of his way and grabbed the hoop.

"I won," Ivan gloated, holding up two of the hoops proudly.

"You pushed Terris, that shouldn't count," Deliah said.

"Hopefully that's good news," Kiernan said. When Lana turned to look at him, he continued, "That's a Council carriage."

She followed his gaze and saw a large white carriage near the stables. It was led by two horses and was draped in gold cloth. The driver jumped out of the seat and opened the door. A man stepped out. He adjusted his cloak before turning to a soldier.

Orin's infectious laughter drew her attention, and she was surprised to see Terris chasing him, also laughing. Deliah was talking to Marnie a few feet away. Dominic, Ivan, Randy, and Carter were throwing the hoops to each other. Maris whistled.

"Everyone over here. We have a lesson to get through."

Lana turned back to the Council messenger, wondering what news he was bringing. He made his way to the castle, escorted by the soldier.

"Can't we have the day off?" Deliah asked. "It's so nice out."

"It is nice out," Maris agreed. "That's why we're going to do our lessons here. Now, before we move on, we wanted to remind you all that it's never too early to begin thinking about your purpose."

Deliah sighed loudly. She sat on the ground with her legs spread out in front of her.

"Who can tell me what your purpose is?" Maris asked. When Orin raised his hand, she turned to him. "Go ahead."

The little boy grinned. "To be king."

Ivan snorted and Maris shot him a warning look. Lana bit her lip, hoping Maris wouldn't ask her what her purpose was. Ever since she had lost the Crystal, she knew what she had to do; she needed to fix her mistake. But she didn't want to talk about it.

Deliah raised her hand. "Well, we all know my purpose. I'm a princess."

At Deliah's words, Lana's stomach coiled. The Crystal was only the beginning, her true purpose was bigger; what she had been sent into hiding for. Her crown was heavy on her head, and she wanted nothing more than to take it off. It wasn't fair that she had been thrust into a life that she didn't want.

She cleared her throat, and everyone turned to look at her. "What happens if your purpose is chosen for you?" Maris narrowed her eyes, clearly not understanding her question and she rushed to continue, "I mean, if your life is predetermined and you have no say."

Terris offered her a weak smile.

"You misunderstand what purpose is," Mrs. DeGette said. "Your purpose isn't your vocation or your responsibilities. Your purpose is what motivates you, what sets your soul on fire. For some people, this can be their vocation. For others, it isn't, and that's okay. Your purpose is why you exist. It's important to begin thinking of this now."

"For me, my purpose is helping others learn," Maris added. "I'm lucky, for my purpose is also my vocation. I wake up every morning excited to meet with you. For others, their purpose could be writing, or drawing. Although their job isn't writing, or drawing, it's what fuels them."

Deliah raised her hand. "How do we find our purpose?"

"Great question," Maris said. "Think about what you enjoy, what you're naturally good at. Ever since I was young, I loved helping others."

"If you didn't have to go to lessons, or work, what would you be doing?" Mrs. DeGette added.

"Sleeping," Ivan said. "That was easy." There was all-round snickering at that.

"I think this would be an excellent assignment," Mrs. DeGette said, ignoring Ivan and looking at Maris. When Maris nodded, she continued, "In addition to finishing your overdue homework, everyone will begin thinking about their purpose. Make a list of things you're good at, things you enjoy, and your greatest accomplishments to date, along with a list of things you would spend your days doing if lessons, or work, weren't forced upon you."

Lana sighed. She still had a paper to finish and wasn't in the mood to think about her motivations. Which category did *fix the biggest mistake of my life* fall under?

"Onto the real lesson," Maris said excitedly. "Let's work on our intuition. There are physical and emotional cues that guide us. The key is to learn how to recognize these cues."

Kiernan elbowed her in the side, and she turned to look at him. He nodded discreetly toward the stables as Maris continued to talk. A soldier was escorting the Council messenger back to the carriage.

"Pay attention to how your body responds in different situations," Mrs. DeGette said.

Lana wondered if the Council was delivering good news. Perhaps they found the Crystal? Or maybe they knew how to find it. She plucked a blade of grass and twirled it in her fingers. Terris nudged her and she looked up, surprised to see Maris standing before her.

"Do you have an answer, Lana?"

She hadn't heard the question, and was going to ask her to repeat it when Nick began laughing. She was instantly transported to Mt. Sinclair. All the times he had picked on her overtook her, a deluge of memories assaulting her.

"Some things never change," he said. "You're just as clueless here."

Ivan laughed but everyone else was silent. Nick stood up and walked toward the castle without another word.

"He doesn't mean that," Terris whispered.

She looked at the grass, away from everyone's prying eyes. Mrs. DeGette followed Nick. Ivan stopped laughing when Maris narrowed her eyes at him.

Maris sighed loudly, knowing that she wouldn't be able to handle all of them alone. "I think we've all had enough. I'm releasing you early. Use the time to finish your homework."

Lana wondered what happened to Nick. Had he gotten in trouble? Would he come back to lessons tomorrow? She realized this was her new normal. Would he ever be nice to her?

"Aw, come on," Dominic sighed. "I'll be working on homework all night."

"Well I'm ending class early, so you have extra time to work on it," Maris countered.

All around them, their classmates were talking about the extra homework assignment, complaining very loudly. Grant caught her eye.

"Sounds like you have a lot of homework tonight," he said.

Lana nodded. She followed him back to the castle, wondering how she was going to write about her purpose when it felt like hers was unattainable.

7

LANA'S DECISION

L ana stared at the blank paper before her. She had finished her assignment on manifesting, but didn't remember what she actually wrote. She was just glad she had something to turn in.

For some reason she was having the hardest time writing about her purpose. She couldn't think of an answer—how could she put into words that she had to fix her mistake? She closed her eyes, tapping a pencil on her palm, rehashing the strange incident in the Square in her mind. How had she made time stop?

She set the pencil on the floor and leaned against the trunk. She closed her eyes and took a deep breath. She thought of Ava and Trevor, and the urge to go to Mt. Sinclair to see them overcame her once again. They would help her make sense of it all.

She looked at the pencil and imagined two hands reaching out and lifting it into the air. To her surprise, it worked. The pencil rose slowly.

There was still a part of her that couldn't fathom magic. Growing up in Mt. Sinclair had been easy. Magic seemed to complicate things, make life difficult.

The pencil flew around the room, dipping and twirling erratically, in subtle imitation of her mood. She drew the pencil toward her and snatched it from the air. She set it down when she heard voices outside of her room. A moment later, a sharp knock broke through the silence.

She made her way to the door, thankful for the break. When she opened it, she was surprised to see Grayson and his brothers.

"How were lessons?" he asked, leading his brothers into the room.

Lana pressed her lips together, thinking of an answer. She wanted to tell him that it had been awful, that she wanted to go back to Mt. Sinclair and forget the last few weeks even happened. She knew that wasn't the answer he was looking for.

"Fine. I'm trying to catch up on homework."

He narrowed his eyes, as if he knew she were lying, when Elijah patted him on the back. "Smart and dedicated. She doesn't pick that up from you Grayson."

"Must have been Jacqueline's influence," Calum added. "She's kept you in line all these years."

Grayson remained silent. She didn't know how to take this sudden uncharacteristic change.

"What was he like growing up?" she asked, walking back to the bed and sitting down.

Elijah laughed. "Grayson was always in trouble."

"Always," Calum agreed, crossing his arms over his chest. "I remember when he ran away and we found him in Cernak Falls."

"He left in the middle of the night. Mom and Dad wouldn't take him. So he went alone. It must have taken him forever to walk there."

Grayson chuckled. "I saw the falls, didn't I?"

Lana couldn't believe what she was hearing. She had always

known him to follow the rules and he made sure she did as well.

"You ran away? How old were you?"

His cheeks flushed. "Fourteen."

"You wouldn't even let me go to out of town football games with Ava and Trevor!"

Calum grinned. "I never would have guessed you were the strict one."

"They were both strict." Lana turned to her father, a wide grin on her face. "I didn't realize all I had to do was run away."

"All right, all right, settle down. That was a long time ago," Grayson said, moving toward the door. "Things are different now. We need to meet up with Jacqueline for dinner. We can't be late."

Calum chuckled. "Yes, you haven't seen her in three hours."

"How are you handling everything?" Elijah asked, turning to her. "I imagine it's been a transition."

That was an understatement. She bit her lip, thinking of everything she had been through in the past few weeks. She would have called it confusing, tumultuous—chaotic even. Instead, she forced a smile.

"It's been fine."

"You're handling it a lot better than I would have," Grayson said softly, sparking quiet nods around the room.

Before she knew it, a tear slid down her cheek. She quickly wiped it away, but more started pouring out. She tried to calm herself, knowing she looked ridiculous. But she forgot about that when Grayson wrapped his arms around her, hugging her tightly. She melted into the hug, taking in all the comfort she could get.

"It's okay," he whispered.

She nodded. He was right. She was going to get through everything—with time.

He pulled away from her and looked into her eyes, his

hands still on her shoulders. "This has all been a big life change. Everything you're feeling is normal."

She nodded and wiped the tears. Both Calum and Elijah were watching them closely. Grayson stepped backward, giving her space. Her reflection in the mirror caught her attention. Her eyes were red, and her skin was paler than usual.

"I'm sorry," she said. "I don't know what came over me."

Elijah frowned. "You don't have to apologize for your feelings."

"You both live in Medora?" she asked a moment later, uncomfortable with the silence that fell over them.

Elijah nodded. "The outskirts."

"My wife and I moved to Medora after Grayson left," Calum said. "Elijah and Cole followed us."

Elijah's face lit up. "Cole's my partner."

"Are they here?"

"We thought it best to meet you first."

Calum crossed his arms over his chest. "Plus, it's hard to travel with five kids."

"You just wanted the break," Grayson teased.

Lana wanted to ask her father if he had met Calum and Elijah's families but didn't know if she was strong enough to hear the answer yet. Her spirits plummeted when she realized the likelihood that he hadn't. She couldn't remember a time that he had been away. There had been no work trips, no visits to out of town family. Her stomach recoiled at the thought that her parents gave up their friends and family, their entire lives, in order to give her a normal life.

"Are you coming, Lana?" Grayson called, pulling her from her thoughts.

All she wanted to do was finish her homework, but knew the break would be good for her. It would be a chance to clear her head. She stood up and made her way to the door.

As they walked, she wondered what it would be like to leave

your home, all of your family, to raise a child that wasn't even yours. A lump formed in her throat and she swallowed, hoping to break its hold on her.

Calum looked back at her as if he sensed her guilt. "Once you're settled in, you'll have to visit us in Medora."

Lana recoiled. She had no desire to visit Medora. Alderic was most likely hiding in the caves, where he had summoned the demons. She imagined Medora as a dark and desolate place and didn't know why anyone would want to live there.

Calum chuckled. "It's not as bad as you think it is."

She smiled, trying to hide her disdain. "What do you mean?"

"The caves are only a fraction of Medora. You have a lot of supporters in the city."

"Maybe I'll visit one day."

She heard boisterous laughter and looked over the railing to find the dining hall full. A few people were even standing outside the doors, talking. She left Grayson and his brothers to make her way inside. She sat at her usual seat.

"Did you finish your homework?" Dominic asked her.

She looked up to find her cousin with his right hand propped on the table. His head was resting in his palm.

"No." She exhaled loudly. "I'm hoping Terris can help me after dinner."

"I still have a lot to finish. We shouldn't have this much homework. I have better things to do."

She nodded, wondering what better things he had to do. Play Parsneakity? Argue with Deliah? It was at that moment she realized her cousin hadn't been sitting next to her brother. She looked around the room, surprised to find her at the next table, talking to Nick.

"Why is she talking to him?"

Dominic turned around, curious to see who she meant. When he saw his sister, he shrugged his shoulders.

"As long as she leaves me alone, I don't care who she talks to."

Lana cared. But before she could say anything, Jacqueline joined them.

"How were lessons today?" she asked, taking a seat.

She was about to answer, but King Ramos appeared behind her. He placed his hand on her shoulder and leaned in.

"Can we talk? After dinner?"

The familiar pit in her stomach returned. She nodded and he stepped away, walking to his seat at the head of the table. She looked at Jacqueline, wondering if she knew what he wanted to talk about, but she only shrugged.

Terris approached them and put a glass of water in front of her. He placed another cup in front of Jacqueline before turning to the cart behind him.

"Can you help me later?" Lana asked. "With my homework?"

"Sure," he said, placing two more glasses on the table for Dominic and Deliah. "After my shift."

An old man with grey hair rushed to the cart. He narrowed his eyes at Terris before turning away with the carafe. He made his way toward the far end of the table.

"I better get back to work."

Lana wondered why Terris insisted on working when Ramos had told him he didn't have to. He had to have better things to occupy his time.

"Where's our water?" Charlotte asked loudly, looking around the room.

Terris took off toward her. She watched her friend hastily fill a glass for the Queen. Charlotte pushed her chair back angrily, hitting him in the knees. The water spilled on her. The color drained from her friend's face when he realized what had happened.

"I'm so sorry," he said. "I didn't mean—"

"Enough," Charlotte spat.

Everyone around the King and Queen had stopped talking, watching the scene unfold. Terris took a slow step backward, unsure what to do. He held out a napkin for Charlotte who grabbed it angrily from his hands.

Terris muttered his apologies again but Charlotte's wrath was only building. When she opened her mouth, presumably to yell at Terris, Lana's eyes narrowed, willing her to remain silent, and like clockwork, Charlotte was rendered mum. Ramos watched his wife, his forehead crinkled in confusion. Charlotte's hands flew to her mouth and Ramos stood, stepping closer to her. He led her outside.

Lana's hands tingled again and went cold. She wiggled her fingers, trying to increase her blood circulation. Her mouth ran dry, and she reached for her water, drinking the entire cup.

"That was weird," Deliah said, sitting next to her brother. "What do you think is wrong with Mom?"

"I don't know," he said.

All around her, the whispers began. She tried clearing her head, making sense of what happened. Charlotte and Ramos walked back into the room but she tried to ignore them. She picked up her fork and felt Jacqueline's intent gaze on her. She turned to look at her, seeing her long fingers clutched around her necklace. When their eyes met, Lana quickly looked away.

"I don't know what came over me!" Charlotte said, speaking very loudly to the woman next to her. "It must be the stress from my travels, and the unpacking."

"Couldn't be the stress from your missing son," Dominic muttered.

Deliah frowned, running her fork along the plate absent-mindedly. Charlotte erupted in laughter over something the woman said. Lana suppressed the urge to silence her again. She wasn't sure how she had done it, and if it would have any unintended consequences.

When Lana finished eating, she quickly stood up and walked into the hall. She heard her parents behind her and knew they were just as eager to find out why her uncle wanted to speak to her. Ramos joined them, gesturing for her to follow. He led them to his office.

The soldiers standing guard bowed to Ramos and Lana as they passed. When the doors were safely closed behind them, he walked to his desk. He set his hands on the table. Sharp silence overtook them.

"I received a message from the Council," her uncle's voice cracked.

Lana held her breath, waiting for him to continue. Had Alderic been captured? Was he imprisoned in the Yards? Had they found the Crystal?

He cleared his throat. "They aren't going to make a statement. They acknowledge that he escaped, and they have their best reapers looking for him."

Lana's breath caught in her throat, and she took a deep lungful of air. Jacqueline took her hand and squeezed it gently.

"I don't understand. Why aren't they going to make a public announcement? With more people looking for him, he'll be caught."

"I agree." He sighed. "They're hoping to have him back before anyone else notices."

"A whole crowd of people saw him," she said, remembering her uncle's birthday party. "There were so many people here. We all saw him."

"I know. It's not my decision to make," Ramos said. "The Council knows what they're doing. We have to trust them."

Her pulse quickened and her face flushed. She couldn't understand why the Council wasn't doing more to find him. Did they even care that he escaped? Were they working with him?

"I think we should send you into hiding again."

The words hung in the air. They were suffocating. What did that even mean? Would she be sent back to Mt. Sinclair? Somewhere else? Would her parents go with her?

"Only until Alderic is caught," he added.

"Who would go with Lana?" Grayson asked.

"You and Jacqueline," Ramos answered, his eyes darting over the papers on the desk. "Grant."

Lana instinctively crossed her arms over her chest, wanting to hold onto something, anything to keep her rooted. She had only learned the truth a few short weeks ago. She had to leave her friends in Mt. Sinclair. She hadn't even been given the chance to say goodbye. She couldn't do it again. When would she see her cousins, or Terris? She didn't want to lose anyone else.

"No."

Lana had been startled by the authoritative tone of her voice. She was tired of everyone but her having a say in her life. She didn't want to leave. She didn't want to start over. What was the point? No matter where she was, Alderic would still find her.

"This isn't up for discussion," Ramos said with an air of finality. "It's what's best for you. As soon as my brother is safely imprisoned in the Yards, you'll come back."

The room began spinning. She closed her eyes and tried to steady her breathing. She knew she had to stand her ground. She had to fight for what was right. She had led both Alderic and Contlay to the Crystal. She had to fix her mistake, and she couldn't do that if she was in hiding somewhere else.

"I'm not going," she said, opening her eyes.

"It's for the best," Grayson said. "Alderic's looking for you. We can go somewhere far away. Where no one knows who you are. You'll be safe."

Ramos held his hand up.

"Why don't you want to leave?"

Her mind raced as she thought of a compelling answer. She was tired of running, of hiding. She wanted everything to be over.

"Am I just going to hide the rest of my life?" she asked. "It seems like we're giving up."

"I know it's a lot, Lana, but it's a good idea," Jacqueline said. "It won't be forever. You'll be safe, protected. Alderic won't know where you are. As soon as he's caught, we'll come back."

"I don't want to hide anymore." Lana turned to her. "I don't want to constantly worry that he's going to find me. You know he'll keep searching."

Ramos met her eyes, and she held his gaze.

"I'm tired of hiding," she repeated. "And I'm not leaving."

The room was quiet. She clenched her hands into balls, pressing her nails into her palms in an effort to steady her nerves. Leaving was out of the equation. She squared her shoulders, projecting an air of false confidence.

"What do you propose we do then?"

Lana was silent. While she knew running wasn't the answer, she didn't know what was.

"We need to do something," she said, her mind working in overdrive, thinking of a plan. "If the Council isn't going to tell people, I will. The more people that know, the better chance we have that he'll be caught."

Ramos looked off in the distance. Her parents were silent, waiting to see what he would say. The look on Jacqueline's face told her that she didn't agree with her suggestion.

"He's building his army," Lana added. "Why can't we build ours?"

Ramos watched her, searching for a seed of doubt. He opened his mouth, as if he were going to say something, but then stopped. He looked at Jacqueline and Grayson.

"What do you think?"

"We should go," Jacqueline said. "She isn't ready for this."

Lana spun around to face her. "Seriously? I can't do this anymore. I want to live a normal life and that won't happen if I'm constantly running."

Jacqueline took her hands. Her fingers wrapped around Lana's.

"I know this has been a lot to take in, but it's for the best."

Grayson cleared his throat. "Jac, she's right. It's not fair. She's old enough to make her own decisions. If she wants to try, we should let her."

Lana pushed Jacqueline's hands off of hers and ran to Grayson. She pulled him in a tight hug.

"Please. Let's at least try. I'll talk to anyone you want. Once they hear our story, they'll help. The more people that are out there looking for him, the better. He'll be caught and sent back to the Yards," she said, her tone earnest.

Lana realized she had been harsh and rested her soft gaze on Jacqueline, silently pleading for her support. She held her breath, waiting for her uncle's decision. He pursed his lips before walking to the opposite side of his desk. He sat down and placed his elbows on the top, steepling his fingers in front of him.

The air felt heavy as she waited with baited-breath. Jacqueline drew closer, taking Lana's hand in hers again. She knew she was only trying to protect her. She looked at Grayson, and the familiar pang of guilt wrapped around her. He had just gotten his brothers back.

"We'll start with King Simon," Ramos finally said, just when she thought she wouldn't be able to handle the anticipation any longer. "If we have his support, it will be easier to secure others. I need you to understand if this doesn't work, you'll be sent into hiding again."

Lana smiled. "Terris should come with us. He was with me that night. The night the Crystal went missing."

Ramos stood with a nod. "I'll speak with him."

She sighed, all the pent up frustration escaping her. While she was excited he agreed to her plan, she was also nervous. She had never met King Simon and didn't know if he would even believe her story. She had no evidence and hoped she wasn't making a mistake.

"We'll leave in the morning," Ramos added. "I'll send a messenger to let King Simon know we're coming."

Ramos walked to the door and her parents followed. Jacqueline looked back at her, smiling weakly when she caught her eye. Even though Lana was worried, she didn't want to live the rest of her life in fear. She hoped King Simon believed her before she was forced into hiding again.

8

PORT MORGAN

They had been traveling for hours and Lana was exhausted. The warm sun found its way through the window, burning her face and making her sleepy. She was so tired her eyes ached, making it hard to keep them open.

The rhythmic sound of the horses' hooves lulled her into an alternate state of mind. It seemed as if she had been riding in the carriage for days and she was starting to feel claustrophobic. Everything was numb, from her toes to her brain.

She leaned against the window, wishing she could be outside with the army instead of riding in the cramped carriage. While she had never ridden a horse, she would have gladly tried, if only to be in the fresh air. She saw Kiernan and his father, Langdon, atop large brown horses. She hadn't been expecting to see him but remembered that he and his father had traveled to Sirmion a few weeks ago to ask King Simon for help against the growing rebel threat. It made sense that they would accompany them.

Kiernan sensed her gaze and waved. She felt her cheeks flush and knew she was blushing. She slid down in her seat, hoping he couldn't see her bright red cheeks through the glass. Her parents had been watching her.

"Are you all right, Lana?" Grayson asked.

"I'm fine."

"Your face is red," he said, sliding across to sit next to her. "Do you have a fever?"

Terris looked out the window, saw Kiernan, and chuckled. She shook her head, but Grayson still reached over and placed his hand on her forehead. She wished he would leave her alone.

She fell back into the seat again, her head resting against the window and her gaze on the clear blue sky. For a moment, she was transported back to Mt. Sinclair. She remembered sitting on her hammock in her backyard, looking at the sky and thinking about her future. She had always imagined going away to college. Even though she hadn't known what she wanted to study, she had looked forward to the freedom.

The carriage came to a halt after a bend in the road. She sat up, wondering if they were already in Sirmion. But when Ramos turned in his seat to look out the window, she could tell he was surprised at the stop too.

A tall man with thinning grey hair was talking to the soldiers. Ander reached into a bag strapped across his chest and handed something to the stranger, who put it in his pocket.

"Winter will be here before you know it." Ramos sighed, sitting back in his seat. "I need to send extra supplies."

Grant nodded, making a mental tab to remind Ramos when they got back to Bridian. Terris leaned close, trying to look out the window. The stranger went from soldier to solider, collecting whatever they gave him.

"Who is that? What's he doing?"

"Everyone isn't as fortunate as we are," Grayson said.

"We had to increase taxes years ago," Ramos explained. "As a result, many businesses closed their doors. Some lost everything. They have a camp out here. I send them supplies every few months —clothes, medicine, and food. It's not a lot. I wish I could do more."

Lana frowned. "What's the winter like here? How much snow can I expect?"

"The winter season is shorter," Grayson said. "A few months of light snow."

The horses' neighs signaled the movement of the carriage. She closed her eyes and memories of Mt. Sinclair assaulted her again. She realized that summer vacation was only a month away. She wondered how Ava and Trevor would spend it.

Last summer, she had plenty of sleepovers with Ava. They stayed up late, telling ghost stories, watching their favorite television shows, and swimming at the public pool. Trevor spent the days with them but went home at night.

She opened her eyes, surprised to see that she was alone in the carriage. She hadn't heard anyone leave. The carriage was slowly making its way forward, although she didn't see any soldiers.

"It's nice to see you again, Lana."

The voice sent a cold shiver down her spine. Alderic. She hadn't heard him enter the carriage and didn't know how he could have. No one else was in sight.

He leaned into the seat and crossed his right leg over his left. He watched her, his lips curving into a wide smile, making his gaunt cheekbones rise. His skin was pale, and his hair was pulled back into a low knot.

"How?"

The word escaped her lips without much thought. He held up his hand, his fingers a hair's length from her face. She jumped to the other seat, putting as much distance as she could between them. Her heart rate increased, and beads of sweat trickled down her forehead. She inhaled a deep lungful of air and steadied her frantic breathing. She needed to calm down, appear strong and in control.

"What did you do? Where did everyone go?"

Alderic uncrossed his legs and bowed forward. "Have you thought about my offer?"

Her mouth ran dry. She turned around and began pounding on the window that looked out toward the front of the carriage. She screamed, hoping to get the attention of the driver. Alderic only laughed.

"There's no one to help you."

"What do you want?"

She slowly turned around and inched her way to the door. If given the opportunity, she would jump out of the carriage. She would do anything to get away from him.

Alderic was aware of her tactic, and stuck his foot in front of the exit. "I just want to talk to my daughter."

"I'm not your daughter." Her voice was cracking. "Leave me alone."

Alderic tilted his head to the left, his brown eyes trained on hers. Her stomach sank when she realized she had his eyes—they were the same color and shape. She really did look like him.

"They're not your parents," he spat, his nostrils flaring. "You were taken from me. I would have raised you. Kalinia would have wanted that."

She didn't say anything. She knew it was pointless. Instead, she sat back in her seat, trying to think of another way out of the carriage.

"Where are they?"

He sighed, his face twisting into a grimace. "Our time together was stolen. I've wondered what you would be like— what you looked like. I'll forever hate Ramos for our separation."

"What did you do to him?"

"Nothing—yet," he answered. "I need you to come with me. To Medora. We can release the demons and take our revenge on those that separated us."

She couldn't believe what he was saying. She had already told him that she would never join him, that she wanted nothing to do with him. Did he honestly think that she changed her mind?

She shook her head. She briefly thought about agreeing—if only to placate him, but couldn't hide her true feelings. She didn't want anything to do with him, his rebels, or the demons.

"He's brainwashed you," he said calmly.

"No one had to brainwash me," she said, trying to keep her voice steady. "I know what's right."

Alderic was silent. He crossed his arms over his chest and looked out the window. She slid ever so slightly closer to the door, praying that he would be distracted long enough for her to escape.

"I'll kill them," he interrupted her plotting. "All of them. Those people you call your parents, my brother, everyone you care about."

Lana couldn't breathe. Her heart was beating so fast within her chest she thought she would pass out. A low ringing echoed in her head, making it hard to concentrate.

He sprang forward and took her by the shoulders, looking deep into her eyes. His nails dug into her skin and she shrieked.

"You care about that boy, Amos and Shandra's worthless son," he continued. "I'll kill him too."

She pushed away from him, but had nowhere to go. The carriage sped up and she gripped the seat, trying to steady herself. Alderic dragged her toward him again.

"Tell my brother I'm always watching."

The carriage jerked, and it felt as if she were being pulled back. A scream escaped her lips. When she opened her eyes, she saw Jacqueline kneeling before her on the floor. She was stroking her hair. Grayson and Ramos were looking down at her too, worry clear on their faces. She sat up and sighed with relief when she saw Terris and Grant safe as well.

"Lana are you okay?" Jacqueline asked. "You were screaming in your sleep."

"It was a dream," she mumbled. "He's not really here?"

Jacqueline frowned. "Who?"

"Alderic. He was here, in the carriage. Everyone else was gone. He wanted me to help him."

Her mother ran her fingers through Lana's hair once more. "It was only a dream."

Her parents exchanged a worried look. Ramos leaned back in his seat and crossed his arms over his chest. Lana didn't know how to explain what had happened. It didn't feel like a dream but she couldn't think of any other way Alderic could have appeared in the carriage. It had felt so real—like he had been right there with her. The carriage stopped.

"Are we there?" she asked.

"We're only in Port Morgan," Ramos said, stepping out of the carriage. "We're staying here tonight."

She followed him outside, grateful for the fresh air. She took in her surroundings. A building sat next to the edge of a cliff. She adjusted her duffel bag on her shoulder while looking at the sign shaking in the wind. *Morgan's Inn* was scrawled in thin letters. She wondered if the Inn, and the town of Port Morgan, had been named after her family.

The crash of waves broke her from her reverie. The smell of the salt water enveloped her, and she took a deep breath, letting it fill her. A light drizzle made her shiver. It was getting cold.

"Everything hurts," Terris groaned. "Do you think we can walk the rest of the way?"

"I'll walk with you," she said.

She wrapped her arms around her chest, still shivering. The party made their way to the Inn. She scanned her surroundings for Kiernan but didn't see him with the soldiers.

The inside led to a large lobby with dark wood floors and low ceilings. A long spiral staircase led to the bedrooms. On the left of the lobby was another room, full of tables.

A man stood near the staircase, talking to Kiernan and Langdon. When they saw Ramos, they stopped talking.

"King Ramos, I trust you had an uneventful journey?" the man said.

"Very much so," Ramos answered.

"I'll show you to your rooms."

The rain picked up, pelting the roof as they made their way up the stairs. The second floor was just as dark as the first. The man led them down the hall to the right, stopping at a closed door.

"Lana, you can take this room. Grant will be in the room across the hall," Ramos said.

She nodded. Even though the day hadn't been physically challenging, she was exhausted. She dropped her duffel bag at the foot of the bed. Jacqueline followed her inside, kissed her forehead, and bid her goodnight.

Lana hugged her parents. She waved goodbye to Terris and closed the door once they left for their own rooms. She walked to the four-poster bed and stood still for a moment, watching the rain drip down the window.

She crashed on the bed and closed her eyes, listening to the strange, almost shallow music of the rain. She used to love listening to music in Mt. Sinclair. It calmed her. She enjoyed putting on her headphones and escaping reality—if only for a few minutes. It was one of the things she missed most in Bridian. There were no headphones, wi-fi, or cellphones to stream music.

She didn't know how much time had passed. One minute she was enjoying the solitude, and the next she heard someone at her door. Terris let himself in. He looked like he had seen a ghost, eyes wide, face pale, and heavy breathing. She got up.

"Everyone had gone downstairs," he said, after catching his breath. "A few minutes later, I heard shouts. I think it's rebels."

The room spun and she gripped the bedpost. Was Alderic here? Seeing him in her dream was one thing, but she didn't think she would be able to face him again so soon.

"We need to leave. Maybe we can escape before they find you."

"Where's Grant? My parents?"

"Outside. They were helping with the luggage. Everyone's outside, Lana. We were ambushed."

Grant had been with her the entire day. What were the odds that the rebels would attack when everyone was outside, leaving her unprotected? How did they even know she was in Port Morgan? A cold chill snaked down her spine when she remembered her dream. Alderic had said he was always watching. It had been more than a dream.

Terris forced her up. She snapped out of her thoughts and ran to the door, grabbing her duffel bag as she passed. She held her breath, listening for any sounds to alert her that someone was in the hall. When she didn't hear anything, she pulled the door open just far enough to slip out.

Before she could ask what he was doing, Terris ran into a room two doors down. A moment later, he was back in the hall, his bag in his hands. He held his forefinger to his mouth and gestured further down the hall, pointing to a dark stairwell.

The lights flickered and she stopped walking. When they came back on, she ran toward the stairwell and bumped into someone.

"Lana?"

She breathed a sigh of relief when she recognized the voice. "Did you see what's going on? Is everything all right?"

"I was coming to get you," Kiernan said, his voice low.

"Everyone was outside. I was going to help when I heard screaming."

She nodded. She knew it couldn't be good. Her parents, Ramos, and Grant wouldn't leave her unprotected if they could help it. Kiernan led them down the stairs into a massive kitchen. He made his way across the room, leading them to a door which led to another stairwell.

What little light there was disappeared when Kiernan closed the door. She put her hands on the wall to keep her balance. A bright ball of light appeared, floating above Kiernan's hands.

"How did you do that?"

"I can't hold it for long," he said. "We need to go."

Lana and Terris ran down the stairs, following Kiernan. As they she reached the bottom, the light disappeared.

Lana fumbled in the dark. "Where are we?"

"We're in the wine cellar. There's a hole in the wall that'll take us to the old Port Morgan."

Lana heard dripping water and shivered. "What do you mean—old Port Morgan?"

"Can either of you give us light?" Kiernan asked, ignoring the question.

"I can't do that," Terris said. "That's magic beyond my capabilities."

Another flicker of light appeared above Kiernan's outstretched hands. As quickly as it appeared, it disappeared. She heard him try again but to no avail. She sensed their eyes on her.

"I've never done anything like that before," she stammered.

"You can do it," Terris said. "You have more magic than anyone I know."

"Call it from within," Kiernan said, leaving her to wonder what that even meant.

She held her hands out in front of her. She imagined a ball

of bright white light several inches above her palms. Her hands tingled. She tried again, but nothing happened. Frustrated, she threw her hands down.

"I can't do this. Everyone expects me to excel at everything. I'm just as clueless as the rest of you!"

Terris and Kiernan were quiet. Even though she couldn't see anything, she knew they were looking at her—or at least in her general direction. She heard a loud crash upstairs and Terris gasped. If they were going to make it out, they needed light.

She held her hands out in front of her again. She was going to try a different tactic. Instead of fear and necessity, she channeled her confidence. She knew she would make the light appear. She had made time stop in Bridian Square. How much harder could creating light be?

As she listened to the dripping water, she imagined a bright white light to guide them to safety. Her hands tingled again, and she heard Kiernan and Terris talking, planning their escape in the dark. She used the sound of their voices to focus and a warmth spread up her hand. Another loud bang echoed from upstairs.

"We need to go," Kiernan said. "They're going to find us."

A spark of light lit up the dark room above her hands. Like a sparkler, a steady spray of flames fell to the floor as the ball of light grew bigger. Kiernan and Terris stepped back, away from the falling flames.

They watched the ball for a moment. A part of her couldn't believe what she was seeing, what she had created. But what frightened her was that she wasn't surprised. Deep down she knew how easy magic came to her.

Kiernan pushed a tall shelf to his right. With a creak, it moved, revealing a hole.

"How do you know about this?" Terris asked.

"Uncle Alba. He owns the Inn. He was my mother's brother," Kiernan said. "I hope he's okay. He was outside too."

"The man that showed us to our rooms?"

Kiernan nodded. He gestured them closer to the hole. The light above Lana's hands had settled, it no longer reminded her of a fire cracker. The edges had rounded, and the ball rotated above her palms in a settled motion. Her arms were beginning to ache from holding them out, but she was too nervous to move them for fear their only light would vanish.

As soon as she stepped into the hole, the temperature dropped, making her shiver. A stale, earthy smell assaulted her nose.

"What's the old Port Morgan?" she asked again.

"Just an old section of the city that used to flood," Kiernan answered. "No one goes down there anymore."

Lana placed one foot in front of the other, carefully traversing the sloped path. She had never been a fan of the dark. In fact, it terrified her, but so did Alderic. She thought of her parents. Were they looking for her?

She heard Kiernan and Terris behind her and focused on their breathing, using it to distract herself from her fears. Kiernan stepped ahead of her as the hill evened out and the tunnel widened.

"There's an exit up ahead," he said.

He sprinted down the corridor, familiar with the route. Terris stumbled and almost fell, but Lana instinctively reached out, holding him up. He straightened, adjusting his cloak. She took a moment to study their surroundings, trying to see where they were. The ball of light flickered, and for a moment, she feared it was going to disappear.

"Over here," Kiernan called.

They followed the sound of his voice to a large stone wall. When they reached him, he placed his hand on the stone and walked to their left, following the wall. At one point, Lana thought she heard something scuttle between her feet and was glad she couldn't see it.

The dank, musty, earthen smell was replaced by salt. She heard the gentle call of the ocean as they stepped around the stone wall. The biggest, brightest full moon she had ever seen greeted them, illuminating the water. It was so beautiful it took her breath away.

Kiernan stepped onto the beach. She was so in awe of the moon, she didn't notice when she dropped her hands to her side, extinguishing the ball of light.

"Where are we going?" Terris asked.

Kiernan didn't answer. He only gestured them to keep walking.

Lana looked up at the moon once more. She filed it away as another subtle difference from Mt. Sinclair. Another reminder that no matter how similar the two worlds appeared; they were very different. Her new home was deceiving—dangerous even and she needed to remember that. She tightened her cloak around her chest as a shiver ran through her. She extracted her gaze from the moon—away from her family and Morgan's Inn.

9
____

WILLOW HOUSE

The waves rolling onto the shore had a hypnotizing effect on Lana. It almost felt as if everything would be all right, as if Alderic and his rebels hadn't found them in Port Morgan, and the magic surrounding her wasn't bubbling up, on the precipice of overflowing, irrevocably changing the world as she knew it.

She inhaled the salty sea air. In an odd way, it invigorated her. She had always loved the ocean. The warm sand curling around her toes calmed her. When she was a young girl, her parents used to take her to the beach every year. Each summer, they would choose a new destination and spend the week picking seashells, sunbathing, and swimming.

They walked the shore for hours. Kiernan and Lana had alternated summoning the light to guide them forward. At the moment, she had two balls hovering around her. She was nervous at how easy the magic was flowing out of her, it felt off.

She adjusted the duffel bag on her shoulder and looked behind her, making sure they were still alone. The beachfront had been deserted, except for a handful of small crabs that scurried between their feet. They seemed to be drawn to the light, and she was beginning to question if they were really crabs, or another species altogether.

"What's on your mind?" Kiernan asked, interrupting her thoughts and breaking their silence.

Before answering, she looked at the water again. She wished she could go swimming. She tried to remember the last time she had swam that didn't involve fearing for her life in Altaris, and realized it was three months ago for gym class in Mt. Sinclair. Nick had made fun of her bathing suit; a blue one piece that he said reminded him of a whale.

"I hope everyone's okay," she said.

"I'm sure everyone's fine," Terris said. "Half the army was with them."

Lana nodded but his platitude did nothing to placate her. From what Terris and Kiernan had seen, the adults had been caught off guard. No one even had a chance to come inside, to warn her. Her parents weren't trained to fight, and even if they were, it had been years since they'd had any practice. She shuddered at what might have happened if Terris hadn't heard the screams. Would she have escaped? Would the rebels have captured her?

"We're almost there," Kiernan said.

"Where is there? We still don't know," Terris said.

Kiernan ran his hands along his cloak, as if he was wiping them. "Willow House... I mean, my house. We'll be safe and my father will think to look for us there."

Her stomach sank, as if her feet had been pulled out from underneath her. She'd forgotten that Kiernan's father had been with her parents and was caught in the fight too. Kiernan must be struggling just as much as her.

When she caught his eye, she offered him a strained smile. They continued walking, mostly in silence. There really wasn't much to discuss until they received news anyway.

The moon slowly faded, sliding into another realm, giving

way to the sun. The crab-like creatures burrowed in the sand. When they no longer needed the balls of light, Lana let them dissolve away—disappearing into oblivion. Her calves hurt, and her feet screamed in agony with every step. She was tired, sore, and sad.

A wooden walkway materialized on their right and Kiernan motioned them to follow the path. They walked through two enormous willow trees, their branches cascading toward the ground as if in mourning. Beyond the trees stood a huge stone house—black shutters lined the windows and green ivy snaked its way to the roof. To the left was a patch of trees, their leaves full, and bright red fruit dangled off the branches.

"This is your house?" she asked in awe.

Kiernan nodded. "When we aren't at the castle."

Before they reached the front of the house, the door opened, and an older woman stepped out. Her grey hair was pulled back into a tight bun and she wore a blue dress. Her face lit up, lips curling into a wide smile when she saw Kiernan. She stood there, her left hand on her chest.

"I didn't know you were coming. Where's your father?" she asked pulling him into a hug.

The woman's gaze moved to Lana and Terris, her smile vanishing at what she saw.

"I'll explain everything," Kiernan said, following her change of heart. "Let's get inside. I'm hungry."

The woman kissed his cheek before ushering them in. Lana followed, relieved to rest her sore feet.

They stepped into a large sitting area. She followed the woman into the hallway, past furniture that looked too hard and uncomfortable to sit on. Kiernan told the woman their story, and Lana used the time to study the house and take stock of their surroundings.

The hallway led to a large, bright kitchen. The woman walked to the fridge and withdrew a glass pitcher.

"You don't know what happened to everyone else?" she asked. "Your father?"

Kiernan shook his head. He drummed his fingers on the table, trying to keep his mind off of everything. The woman passed a cup to Lana.

"You must be our Princess. Welcome to Willow House. It's lovely to meet you. You can call me Laurel."

"This is my grandmother," Kiernan added, looking up from his own cup.

The woman nodded. "I'm Langdon's mother."

Lana bit her lips nervously. She hoped the woman before her hadn't lost a son, and Kiernan a father.

"It's nice to meet you."

"This is Terris," Kiernan added. "He's a friend."

Terris sat up and smiled, but didn't say anything. Lana played with Kalinia's ring, twisting it around her finger. Her mouth was dry and scratchy; she reached for her glass and took a big sip. The cold liquid quenched her thirst but also made her shiver.

Laurel stood up and walked to the fridge again. She rummaged inside, moving containers to the counter. Kiernan was still drumming his fingers on the table. When he saw that Lana was watching, he put his hands in his lap.

Lana played with her ring again. It was becoming a nervous tic, something to keep her mind off all the bad things going on around her. When a bell rang, she jumped, nearly falling out of her chair.

"Someone's working on the gazebo," Laurel said, wiping her hands on a cloth. "I'll be right back."

Lana's heart rate increased slightly. Were they still safe? Were the rebels here?

Kiernan stood. He walked to the counter. How could he be so calm? Terris was looking at a large painting behind her. She followed his gaze to see what was so fascinating about it. It was dark, lots of midnight blues and black—beautiful, but it felt out of place in the bright, airy kitchen.

"My mother painted that," Kiernan said, looking up from the counter. "Before she died."

She wondered why his mother had created something so dark. She jumped in her seat, startled by the barest of noises. Kiernan had brought a tray of various slices of cheese, crackers, and jam and laid them on the table. Lana's stomach rumbled and she reached for a cracker, hoping it would help settle her nerves. She studied the painting again, trying to gain any insight into the woman who had painted it.

"All set," Laurel came in a moment later. "Why don't the three of you rest for a bit. I imagine you're tired. I'll make dinner."

"That would be great," Lana said, sliding her chair out and standing. "Thank you. I think I need to lay down."

Kiernan stood. "I'll take them to the guest rooms. Maybe Dad will be back before dinner."

Laurel smiled sadly. To Lana, it looked as if it were forced. Kiernan led them back to the front door. When they were in the large sitting room, he made his way to the staircase.

Kiernan turned right on the second floor and led them down the dark hall. A moment later, he opened a door. "Lana, this will be your room. Terris will be right next door."

She stepped past him. A large bed lay next to glass doors that opened onto a deck. The room had a sitting area with a loveseat and chairs nestled around a stone fireplace. A large crystal chandelier hung from the ceiling, casting a rainbow of light around the room.

"The bathroom's across the hall," he added.

Lana didn't know what to say. The room was beautiful, and she was grateful to be safe—out of the elements and hidden from Alderic, but she was worried about her family. She knew he was too. She would have loved to be at his family house in any other situation and the irony wasn't lost on her.

"My room is the third door on the left," he added, turning back to the hall. "Let me know if you need anything."

Once the boys left, she unzipped her duffel bag, looking for clean clothes when Laurel walked in.

"If you leave your dirty clothes in the hall, I'll wash them for you."

She nodded. "Thank you."

Laurel turned to leave and then paused. "I'm glad you're here—safe."

Lana didn't say anything. She wasn't even sure what to say. Laurel smiled one last time and walked into the hall, closing the door behind her.

A light drizzle of rain hit the windows. She gathered her clean clothes and went to the bathroom. Once she was showered and dressed, she brushed her teeth and walked back to the room, leaving her dirty clothes on the floor as Laurel instructed. She jumped into bed and closed her eyes.

Hours later, when she awoke, it took a moment for her brain to register where she was. As everything came crashing to her, filling her memories, her stomach sank. She looked out the unfamiliar window. At least it had stopped raining.

She snuggled back into the covers. Her eyes were heavy, as if the sleep she so desperately needed hadn't been enough. Her body wanted more, craved more, but her mind was on overdrive. What had happened to her parents? Was Ramos all right? Would Kiernan's father bring them here? Would she see her cousins again?

A knock on the door ripped her from her thoughts. She climbed out of bed. She stopped at the antique-looking mirror. She touched the cool surface, relieved when she found it wasn't a portal. She didn't think she would ever look at mirrors the same.

"Lana?" Kiernan's voice called from the other side of the door. "Are you up?"

She made her way to the door, gripping the handle and opening it a little too eagerly. It flung back and hit her foot.

Kiernan looked at the floor, trying to hide his smile as she bent down in pain. Her cheeks flushed and she closed her eyes. She wanted to hide, to crawl back into bed and forget how uncoordinated she could be.

"That looked like it hurt."

She opened her eyes and stood up. "I'm fine. Please tell me you have good news."

He took a deep breath before reaching down for something hidden from her view behind the wall. When he stood back up, he had a wicker basket in his hands. He held it out to her.

"Your clothes. My grandmother washed everything for you."

She reached for the basket, flinching when her hands touched his, and placed it on the floor near her feet.

"How are you?" she asked.

He ran his hand through his hair. "I'm fine. I know he'll be okay. Everyone will be here soon; they're probably just waiting until the threat has passed before..."

The way his voice cracked made her question if he was being sincere. Did he really believe that or was he just trying to make her comfortable? She crossed her arms over her chest and looked toward the hall, wondering if Terris was awake.

"Can I show you something?"

She looked back at him, meeting his eyes. "Sure," she answered, her voice breaking too.

She walked closer to the door, ready to follow him, but he didn't move. "You'll probably want your cloak."

Lana removed her cloak from the basket of laundered clothes. "Where's Terris? Is he coming?"

"He's in the library," he answered. "It'll just be us."

Lana wondered what her friend was doing in the library. She walked to the bed and reached for her duffel bag. She rummaged around in it until she found the drawings. She put them in the front pocket of her jeans. She was hoping to find a moment to study them later. Maybe a fresh perspective would help her decipher their secrets.

She followed him out of the room, closing the door behind her. He led her downstairs, through the empty kitchen and into the backyard. Tall green trees, their trunks camouflaged by their drooping branches, surrounded the property. The bright flowers in the garden looked fake, as if painted on the stalk.

Kiernan led her into the lush garden. The flowers were taller than she was used to in Mt. Sinclair, and it felt like they were in a maze. They followed the stone path to a white bench in front of a large mausoleum.

A light breeze pushed strands of hair into her face. She looked at the sky, wondering if it was going to rain again. Kiernan sat, clasped his hands in front of him and looked at her expectantly.

"I like to come here when I'm home," he said, breaking the silence that had descended upon them.

She looked around, pausing when her gaze fell on a bright purple flower. Thin yellow lines crisscrossed on the petals.

"It's beautiful. Who planted all of these?"

"My mom."

Lana pressed her back against the bench, waiting for him to continue. It seemed as if he wanted to talk, but couldn't find the right words.

"She died when I was ten," he continued. "She was sick for so long. It was almost a relief."

Another burst of wind blew around them. When it settled, he was looking straight ahead, lost in memories.

"I'm sorry."

She wasn't sure what else she should say, or if she should

even say anything. She couldn't imagine the pain of losing someone so close. She had been so young when her birth mother had been murdered. She hadn't been given a chance to know her—to love her. Life could be cruel. She thought of all the evil in the world, all the tragedies people endured. What was the point of it all?

"I didn't mean to make you sad," he said. "I just don't know what I'll do if I lose him too."

Lana wanted to comfort him, but it was too close to home. The same thoughts had been haunting her about her parents.

"He's okay. I know it."

She wished she believed herself. What would she do if something happened to both her parents? Or Ramos? She sank deeper into the bench. If something happened to her uncle, she would be Queen of Bridian. Her head pulsed with a heartbeat all its own.

"There's something I've wanted to tell you," he said.

She looked at him, waiting for him to continue, pushing aside all thoughts.

"When we first met..." he began and then stopped, thinking of what to say. He clasped his hands together, squeezing them tightly. He took a deep breath. "My father instructed me to introduce myself to you. He told me to get to know you."

"Why?" she asked.

He frowned. "When he heard you were back, he thought it would be a good idea for me to meet you, to gain your trust. That's why I asked you to go to Poklin's with me. I've wanted to tell you because I feel guilty, like we started off wrong and I don't want there to be any secrets between us."

"So, you never really wanted to get to know me?"

"It's not like that."

When he didn't elaborate, she asked, "Why? I don't understand. Why did he want you to get to know me?"

When he looked up, his eyes were watery.

"I'm training to take over for him," he said. "As an advisor to Bridian—to King Ramos... and one day, you."

Large grey clouds covered the sky, blocking the sunlight. A strong gust of wind blew past them, chilling her to the bone. She should have known that he wouldn't have actually wanted to get to know her. She should have realized that he seemed a little too eager to take her to Poklin's. Why had she thought Bridian would be any different than Mt. Sinclair?

"I'm sorry," he apologized. "I should have told you sooner."

Lana stood. "I should find Terris."

He nodded. She walked back to the house, questioning her entire life. How could she have believed that he had actually liked her?

Lana's stomach lurched. It felt as if her insides were twisting into knots and she stumbled. Kiernan reached for her arm and held her upright, his eyes narrowed at her.

"I don't know what came over me," she said. "I think it's just stress. I'm fine."

He watched her, waiting to see if she was okay. She pulled away from him.

"I'm fine. Really, I am."

The pain in her stomach dissipated as they made their way back to the house.

Kiernan closed the door behind them and said, "Thanks. For sitting with me, I mean. I really miss her."

She was silent. She didn't know what to say. She needed time to process what he told her.

"I like you, Lana." Kiernan's voice cracked. "I just wanted you to know so that we could start fresh. Maybe I shouldn't have."

"I'm glad you did."

He opened his mouth to say something, but then thought better of it. He looked toward the kitchen and she followed his gaze. Laurel was at the stove, her back to them.

"I'm going to see if she needs any help. The library is down the hall," he said, pointing to their left. "I imagine Terris is still there."

Lana quickly turned around and made her exit. Dark paintings hung on the wall and she wondered if Kiernan's mother painted them. She stood before the largest one, studying it. A violet flower, yellow streaks on the petals, was the focal point. Black paint was circled around the flower, some sections thicker than others.

She stepped away from the painting and saw an open door to her left. The smell of books assaulted her when she stepped inside. The library was smaller than she was expecting. Glossy dark brown shelves lined the walls, all filled with books of various sizes. A large table stood in the middle of the room where she found Terris, his back to her.

As she made her way to him, she felt the sharp pain in her stomach again. She gasped. Terris jumped, startled by the noise. She took another step forward and felt another sharp stab, tearing at her from the inside. It was so intense she collapsed to her knees and screamed when another wave of pain coursed through her. She could think of no other way to describe it, other than something was trying to claw its way out of her stomach. She felt his hands on her back.

The room began spinning and she closed her eyes. Her heart hammered in her chest when she realized she wasn't at Willow House any longer.

10

THE EMPTY LOCKER

Lana found herself back in Mt. Sinclair High School. Mr. Jones had his back to the class, writing on the chalkboard. Nick was sitting to her left, looking out the window. The rest of the class was quiet—taking notes, doodling, and shuffling through their textbooks.

She looked at her open notebook. It was blank. Her bare arm caught her attention. Her cloak had been replaced by the standard Mt. Sinclair High School navy-blue pants and short-sleeved white shirt. She looked at her feet—white sneakers—definitely not what she had been wearing moments ago.

Mr. Jones was still at the chalkboard, his right arm poised, twirling the chalk in his hand, as if he was pondering what to write next. She turned to Nick. She needed to talk to him. Maybe he knew what happened.

She cleared her throat, hoping it would catch his attention. Lisa DeMarco turned to her. She narrowed her eyes, her lips turning into a scowl. Nick focused on his textbook.

She tore a small piece of paper from the notebook and crumpled it into a tiny ball. When no one was looking, she launched it at him. The paper hit his arm, bouncing to the ground. He turned around, looking for the offender.

He saw her watching him and said, "Mr. Jones, Lana is distracting me. She threw a piece of paper at me."

Everyone turned to look at her. Mr. Jones faced the class for the first time, his eyes stopping at Lana. Her cheeks flushed. Nick leaned over the side of his desk to pick up the crumbled paper.

"Here it is," he said, holding it up for all to see.

"She was making noises too. I can't concentrate with her disrupting us like this," Lisa added, throwing her pencil on the desk.

"I only cleared my throat."

"All right." Mr. Jones placed the chalk down. "Lana, did you throw the paper at Nick?"

She bit her lip, thinking of an excuse. Everyone was still watching her, much more interested in the drama than the lesson.

"Lana?"

Nick snorted. He turned to Lisa and asked, "You saw that, right? She threw it at me."

Lisa nodded.

"It was an accident," Lana said, looking back at Mr. Jones. "I didn't mean to hit him."

"What were you aiming for?" Nick asked, not ready to give it up. "Cooper?"

Cooper Gibson was sitting in front of Nick. She hadn't seen him a moment ago. She looked around the room again, trying to think. She didn't remember Cooper being in her music class.

"No," she stammered. "I don't know what happened."

She heard a few chuckles and sank into her chair. She should have known that Nick wouldn't help her. Thankfully, the bell rang, signaling their lunch hour.

"Lana," Mr. Jones called over the class rushing to gather their belongings. "I need to speak with you."

She threw her notebook into her bag. Nick walked past her. He shifted his backpack to his other shoulder exaggeratedly, hitting her in the process.

"Sorry, Laughs."

He walked out of the classroom, his friends snickering at her. She turned to make her way toward Mr. Jones and bumped into Cooper. Her head seemed heavy, as if a dark cloud had expanded, fogging her memory.

"Have you always been in this class?"

"Um, yeah," he said, looking at her as if she had sprouted two heads.

"Lana," Mr. Jones called.

"I'll see you at lunch," Cooper said. "I have to talk to Mrs. DeWitt about my paper."

He smiled before making his way out the door. She let Lisa pass before walking to the front of the classroom. Mr. Jones had papers spread in front of him, writing furiously on one.

"Is something wrong?" he asked, looking up. "You're usually so quiet."

"Yeah. I'm sorry. I didn't mean to hit him."

He went back to the papers, flipping through them. She saw drawings, eerily similar to those she had found in Poklin's and gasped. He gathered them into a pile and threw them into a drawer.

Without looking up, he said, "You're free to go."

"That's it?" she asked. "I'm not in trouble?"

"Not unless you want to be. Think of this as your warning."

"What were those papers?"

He pushed his chair backward. Her mouth ran dry as his eyes trained on her. She wanted to leave.

"Nothing you need to be concerned about. You're going to be late for lunch."

She felt vibrations in her pocket. Her cell phone. She didn't want to remove it in front of Mr. Jones. She turned on her heel and ran to the door. When she was in the hallway, she took it out. Ava's name greeted her, and she opened the message.

Where are you?

Lana threw the phone back into her pocket and made her way to her locker. It wasn't far and she was eager to talk to Ava and Trevor. Maybe they could help her figure out what was going on.

Had she lost her mind? How could she forget going back to Mt. Sinclair? She remembered the pain as she made her way to Terris at Kiernan's house. The pain had been so intense, almost as if she were burning from the inside out. She remembered falling to the floor, but that was it. Try as she might, nothing else came to her.

She took a deep breath as another thought hit her like a ton of bricks. Was she dead? Her hands flew to her cheeks and she touched them, trying to feel if anything was different. She moved down to her arms and touched her legs, but everything felt normal.

When she turned the corner, she saw her friends leaning against her locker. Ava's long black hair was in a loose topknot, strands framing her face. She had a white sweater tied around her waist. Trevor looked up at her, running his hand through his short brown hair.

"There you are," he called out. "What took you so long?"

"I'm so glad to see you," Lana ran toward them. "I've missed you so much."

Her friends looked at each other, a bewildered expression on their faces. When no one said anything, Trevor shrugged. She looked at him, realizing his usually wrinkled clothes were ironed to perfection.

"I don't know what's going on or how I got here. One

minute I was with Terris, you remember him, right?" She didn't wait for them to answer. "The next, I'm sitting in music class."

"Terris?" Ava asked quizzically, as if the name was foreign to her. "Lana, what's going on? Why are you acting so strange?"

With shaking hands, Lana spun the dial on her locker, saying the numbers aloud in her head as she went.

13-10-25

When the lock clicked, she swung the door open. It was empty. She closed it and looked at the number—252. It was her locker, but everything was gone.

"Are you okay?" Ava asked.

"Everything's gone," she mumbled, swinging the locker open again. "All my pictures, my books, even my whiteboard. I mean, I guess it makes sense. I've been gone for a few weeks now."

"What are you talking about?" Ava asked, worried now. "Where did you go?"

"What do you mean? I've been gone for almost a month."

Trevor's mouth fell open and Ava crossed her arms over her chest. Something was very wrong. Lana put her hands on her forehead, trying to think clearly. She remembered the stomach pain. She remembered falling to the floor. How had she wound up in Mt. Sinclair?

Except, she wasn't in Mt. Sinclair, at least the Mt. Sinclair she knew. Things were off—different. Cooper hadn't been in her music class, Nick was in Bridian, with his mom, and Ava and Trevor were acting as if they didn't know she had been gone, as if they had never met Terris.

"So anyway," Ava said, holding out her hands, wiggling her long fingers. "How does this polish look for tonight?"

"I thought you were going with purple," Trevor asked. "Something about matching your dress."

Ava sighed. "They didn't have the right shade. Lana, how do they look?"

She looked down at Ava's nails. They were painted in a French tip—each ring finger had a vertical line of silver glitter running down the nail. They were pretty, but she had more important things to worry about.

"They look great," she said, slamming her locker door shut. "I need to go."

She had only taken a few steps when she saw someone she never wanted to see again coming around the corner. Contlay was wearing a janitor's uniform, pushing a cart full of cleaning supplies. He stopped walking and stared at her.

"You should be in the cafeteria," he said, stepping around the cart.

Lana stepped backward, nearly tripping on her feet. What was he doing here? Why was he dressed like a janitor? He no longer worked for the school.

"We're on our way," Ava said, popping a piece of gum in her mouth. "Come on, Lana. We need to talk about the dance."

Trevor reached for her arm, leading her toward the cafeteria. She turned back to Contlay and saw him watching her, still standing at the foot of his cart. She followed Ava and Trevor to a table near the window, overlooking Lake Sinclair.

"This isn't where we usually sit," she said.

Ava tossed her bags on the table and sat down. "This little game you're playing isn't funny."

Lana looked around the cafeteria, noticing a few subtle differences. The door to the courtyard was on the opposite side of the window. The table where they usually ate was gone. In its place was a station to return used trays. A large poster was taped to the wall, advertising the end of year formal.

Trevor sat down and looked up at Lana, watching her curiously. Before she had a chance to sit, Laurie Huntington waltzed to the table, sitting next to Trevor. He placed his arm around her shoulders. Laurie giggled and Lana's mouth gaped open.

Laurie looked up at her. "Why are you standing?"

She didn't answer. She didn't even know what to say. Laurie turned to her purse, rummaging in it and withdrawing a gold tube of lip gloss. She ran it along her lips and replaced the top before turning to Trevor.

"What time are you picking me up?"

He grinned. "We already went over this. I'll be there at six."

Cooper and Nick came up behind her. Nick sat next to Ava, placing a soda can in front of her. Cooper remained standing by Lana, his head cocked to the side, watching her.

"Are you going to sit?"

Ava giggled. "I don't know what's wrong with her today."

Cooper sat down next to Trevor, patting the space to his left. "I know you didn't want to go to the formal, but now you don't want to sit next to me?"

She sat down, placing her book bag on the floor and turning to Cooper. "We're going to the dance together?"

"Last I knew," he answered, taking a sip of soda. "You were acting strange in music."

"Hey, sorry about that," Nick said, looking at her. "I hope I didn't get you in trouble. What did you want?"

Her breath caught in her throat. Why was Nick all of the sudden acting like they were friends? Why was he sitting next to Ava? He had picked on Ava just as much as her. Laurie laughed as Trevor whispered something in her ear. He had the biggest crush on Laurie, but she had never given him the time of day.

Ava popped the tab on the soda can. "What happened?"

When Lana didn't answer, Nick said, "I think Lana was bored. Either that, or she was trying to get Cooper's attention."

"She always has my attention," Copper said with a wink.

"Hey, do you want a ride home later?" Nick asked, looking at her. "My mom's picking me up."

"Me?" Lana questioned, pointing to herself in disbelief.

Nick picked up another fry and shoved it in his mouth. "Seriously, what's wrong with you? Are you sick?"

Lana couldn't take it anymore. This felt wrong. She remembered all the times that Nick picked on her. She couldn't believe that any version of herself would ever be friends with him.

"Why are you sitting with us?" she asked. "Why is she sitting with us?" she added, pointing to Laurie.

Laurie rolled her eyes. "Rude."

Cooper leaned close. "Maybe you should go see Mrs. Mitroni. Do you want me to take you? I know you've been stressed trying to keep up with your homework and cheerleading."

"Cheerleading?" she gasped. "I'm on the cheerleading squad?"

It was at this moment she knew she was dreaming. Or had she slipped into another universe? An alternate reality perhaps—one where she was popular, where she hadn't been a Princess of Bridian, or at least didn't know it yet.

Ava sighed. She leaned over Nick and grabbed a fry, popping it into her mouth. Trevor wrapped his arm around Laurie again, shaking his head. Cooper was still leaning close to her, his eyes searching hers.

Growing up in Mt. Sinclair, this is the reality she had always wanted. She envied Laurie's popularity. Now that she had it, even if it was only a dream, or an alternate reality, all she wanted to do was wake up. She didn't want to be in Mt. Sinclair, not with these versions of Ava and Trevor. She looked at Cooper, realizing that even this version of Cooper wasn't right. He seemed different, a copy of the person that she had once liked.

She closed her eyes, willing herself to wake up. When she reopened them, she was dismayed to see she was still in the cafeteria. Everyone was watching her, waiting to see what she was going to do, or say, next.

She looked around once more, not even sure what she was searching for. When she stood up, Cooper took her arm.

"I'm going home," she said.

He nodded. "I'll pick you up later? At six?"

"Sure," she agreed, grabbing her book bag and making her way toward the doors.

"What was all that about?" Nick asked, not bothering to wait until she was out of earshot.

Lana didn't wait around to hear their answer. She walked through the doors and made her way down the hallway. She threw open the door at the main entrance, relieved she hadn't seen Contlay, or anyone else for that matter.

When she stepped outside, the warm sun wrapped around her. She ran down the steps and disappeared into the parking lot, making her way between the cars. Without looking back, she crossed the street. With each step she felt a weight lift off her shoulders, as if she could breathe again.

She ran past the creepy house on the corner of Main Street and Portobello Drive. Just before reaching the Mt. Sinclair Welcome Center she entered Frazier Woods. She stopped and looked behind her, almost expecting to see Contlay. She followed the path to Capshaw Creek, only stopping once at the spot that Marty and his accomplice had attacked her.

She had to figure out how to get back and hoped her parents would be able to help. At least, this version of her parents. Even though Ava, Trevor, Nick, and Cooper looked the same, they weren't the same people she knew. These were strangers, masquerading as friends. Would her parents be different as well?

She made her way up Crescent Ave. Her house was on the left. She crossed the street and ran to the front door. She tried the handle, but found it locked. She rang the doorbell and placed her backpack on the railing. She needed to find her keys. When she unzipped the bag, she wasn't surprised to find it empty.

She tossed the empty book bag into the bushes and made her way down the driveway to the backdoor. She saw her parents' car parked in front of the garage and slowly walked up to it. She ran her hands along the side, wondering what was happening to her. The glint of silver caught her eye, and she was surprised to see keys in the ignition. She threw open the door, sighing with relief when she saw the house key.

Suddenly, she heard a strange caw. She watched a crow circle the air above her, as if it was watching her, waiting to see what she would do next. Lana kept one eye on the crow as it followed her to the front door. She inserted the key in the lock and pushed the door open slowly, only to be greeted by the brightest light she had ever seen. She covered her eyes, trying to shield them. A moment later, two hands reached out, wrapping around her waist and pulling her into the light.

11

THE CAVERNS OF MEDORA

When Lana regained consciousness, she was in a dark room lying on her back. The floor beneath her was cold, sending chills up her body. She sat up with some difficulty, everything sore.

"About time you woke up."

She strained her eyes, trying to see who was with her. A tiny window let in a sliver of light, but it wasn't enough to identify who was in the shadows. The voice was familiar, but she couldn't place it.

"You've been asleep for hours," the man said.

A lump formed in her throat. Was she still dreaming?

"Who are you? Where am I?" she asked, tightening her cloak around her body.

The man stepped forward, into the ray of light from the window, and she gasped. Alexander. He looked tired—deep bags lined his eyes, and his face was pale. He was wearing a dirty robe. It didn't look like he had showered since the rebels excavated him from his grave. He was still covered in dirt.

"They took him," he said, his mouth quivering. "Amos never

wanted him. Shandra didn't either. I should have taken him, raised him away from all of this."

He trailed off, mumbling to himself. She tried to wrap her head around everything, but nothing made sense. The last thing she remembered was being in Mt. Sinclair. Where was she now? Who was he talking about?

"You have to get him back," he said, looking up at her again. "Please, you have to save him. I don't care what happens to me —what they do with me. You have to save him."

"Terris?" she asked, her mind racing. "What happened? Where is he?"

Alexander stopped pacing and turned to her. "He came with you. Alderic has him."

The room began spinning. She focused on her breathing, trying to make sense of it all.

"Where am I?"

A look of pity crossed his face. "Medora. He pulled you here."

"I don't understand. Pulled me here? What does that even mean? How did Terris get here?"

"I don't know," he answered, wringing his hands. "He took him."

While she didn't understand what was happening, or how she was in Medora, she knew she wasn't dreaming. She couldn't explain how she knew. All she was certain of was she had to find her friend.

"How do we get out of here?"

"I don't think there's a way out," he said. "His followers are everywhere."

As if to prove his point, the door suddenly opened, bathing the room in light.

"Ah." Damon waltzed in the room. "Good, you're awake. Your father's waiting for you."

Her cousin looked thinner than the last time she had seen

him—right before he jumped out of the window in the abandoned hall. She didn't know how she felt about seeing him standing right in front of her.

"Nice to see you cousin," he added, smiling widely. "I do hope you're feeling refreshed after that nap. Your father mentioned he gave you a nice dream. Something about being back in Mt. Sinclair. He wanted to make you comfortable."

Lana didn't think she had heard him correctly. How could Alderic influence her dreams? "What do you mean?"

Damon crossed his arms over his chest. "Is it really that hard to comprehend? Am I talking too fast?"

Her stomach churned. A part of her had hoped that he would have come to his senses by now—that he would want to come home. Alexander shrunk back, afraid.

"Damon, you have to help me," she pleaded. "I don't know how I got here. Terris is here. I need to find him."

"Terris is here." Damon nodded. "He's safe. For now."

Lana watched from the corner of her eyes as Alexander prepared to move. Damon hadn't seen the brief twitch in his legs and it came as a surprise when he sprang forward, colliding into him. They fell to the floor, but Alexander was no match for Damon in his weakened state. Damon easily threw him off.

"Well, that was unnecessary." He sighed emphatically, then walked up to Alexander who was still laying on the floor, struggling for air. "You're going to pay for that later," he added, kicking him.

Lana's hands flew to her mouth. She wanted to scream for help, but even if someone heard her, it wouldn't matter. She was surrounded by rebels.

"Best not to keep your father waiting," Damon added, looking back at her.

He held his arm out, inviting her to take it.

"I'm not going with you."

Damon frowned. Alexander groaned, unable to get up. Anger flashed across her cousin's face.

"That's too bad. I believe your friend will be joining him."

Lana balked. The quickest way to get to Terris would be to go with Damon. He smiled, seeing the change in her countenance. He knew he had struck a nerve.

"Fine," she said. "Lead the way."

Damon stepped into the hall. He turned back to Alexander. "You better hurry. You know he doesn't like to wait."

Alexander stood up with considerable effort. Damon began walking, leading her through the long hall. She ran to catch up to him.

"Damon, wait." He didn't stop but slowed enough for her to keep up. "It's not too late," she pleaded. "Help me find Terris and let's get out of here. Your father misses you."

He snorted. "You can't be serious. I don't care about him."

He picked up the pace to avoid any more conversation. She struggled to keep up with him. It surprised her that the hall was so empty. Where were the rebels? She looked back and saw Alexander struggling behind them.

"We need to help him. He can't keep up."

Damon only laughed in response. When they came upon an elaborate staircase, he stepped back, allowing her to pass first. She made her way down the steep stairs. At the foyer, the staircase continued off to her right, descending deeper into the house. Thankfully, Damon walked past her to the left. She didn't want to be anywhere near Alderic's dungeons. She followed him through the empty hall. Even though Alderic was the last person she wanted to see, she needed to find Terris, so she kept pace with her cousin.

Damon stopped at an arched doorway. Flowers were carved into the wood. He pushed the door open unceremoniously, gesturing for her to step inside. A long table was placed underneath a crystal chandelier. Crystal sconces lined the walls. A large window stood on the far wall, flanked on either side by heavy drapes. Sunlight poured in through the window, illuminating the table.

The door closed behind her and she jumped. Her heart was racing so fast it hurt to breathe.

"Sit," a cold, but calm voice said.

A shiver went through her. Alderic was sitting at the head of the table. How had she missed him?

"I'm fine here."

Before she had even finished her sentence, he was standing before her. She jumped, tripping over her feet and falling. He offered his hand but she pushed herself backward, moving further away.

"How did you do that?"

He smiled. "Now that I'm free from that *place* I can use magic again. You can do it too. How do you think you got here?"

She shook her head, not understanding the words coming out of his mouth. He had been sitting at the table only a moment ago.

"I can't do that," she stammered.

"You can do so much more." He stepped closer. "You just need to learn to harness the power flowing through you. One of the gifts you've been given is teleportation. I tapped into that gift, the magic, and pulled you to me. We have great things to accomplish."

"No," she said. "I'm not doing anything with you. What did you do in Port Morgan? To Ramos? Were you following us?"

"I did nothing. I wasn't even there."

"What did *they* do to my parents? Your followers?"

His face fell and she knew she had made a mistake. She hadn't meant to say it. She hadn't meant to ask about her parents. The words flew out of her mouth before she could even process them. He ran his hands through his hair and took a deep breath.

"They're not your parents," he said, wringing his hands. "He's not your father. I AM!"

She flinched. Even though she had expected his outburst, his anger shocked her.

"I'll never forgive Ramos for tearing you from me," he continued. "He tore my family apart."

She bit her lip, not wanting to anger him further. It took all of her resolve to remain silent. He was delusional. How could he blame his brother for his actions? It didn't make sense.

"Ramos should have known something would happen." He smiled widely. "I told you to tell him that I was always watching."

He smiled insidiously and walked back to the table. She remembered the dream she had in the carriage on her way to Port Morgan. Alderic had told her to tell Ramos that he was always watching him.

"That wasn't just a dream?"

"It was the only way I could see you at the time," he said, his tone flat. "I needed my magic to strengthen. Your mind is relatively easy to influence."

"Stay out of my head."

He sat in his chair. "Sit."

She shook her head, ignoring his command. "How did you bring me here?"

"The Revatto's magic flows through me," he answered. "Through you. I can't do it all the time if that's what you're wondering. Now, join me. We have much to discuss."

Lana held his gaze. "Where's Terris?"

"Not now. We have other matters to talk of first. I need you to help me find the Crystal."

"You took it! How would I know where it is?"

As the words escaped her mouth, she realized she was wrong. He didn't have the Crystal. Contlay must have it. He wouldn't be wasting his time with her now if he had any inkling where it was.

"You don't have it, do you?"

He shook his head, as if answering were too painful. She took a tentative step closer to the table.

"You're connected to them," he said a moment later. "The demons. I tethered you to them. Now that your magic is awakening, now that you're free from that other place, you can find it."

"I won't help you." She crossed her arms over her chest. "I'm glad you don't have it."

His eyes grew wide. He slammed his fists on the table and stood up. She braced herself, waiting for his attack, but nothing came. She opened her eyes. He was now pacing before the window.

"Sit down," he said, gesturing to the chair at the other end of the table. "Your friend should be here soon."

She couldn't believe what she heard. Was he really going to bring Terris to her? Moments ago, he was so angry. Now he looked calm. He had his back to her, still looking out the window.

"Terris?" she asked hopefully. "Will you let him go?"

He walked back to his chair. When he was sitting, he looked at her, waiting for her to join him.

Lana spun around as the door opened. She watched Alexander make his way toward Alderic slowly, carrying a silver tray. His hands shook when he placed a teacup in front of him.

"Lana, you remember Alexander."

"Why are you doing this? Let him go."

"It's because of him that I was imprisoned in the Yards. It's only fitting that he remain here to serve me."

"You were sent to the Yards because you're evil. You murdered innocent people. You murdered your father."

"Sit down," he snapped. "I will not ask again."

She shook her head. The last thing she wanted to do was sit at the table with him. He had to know she would never work with him. She would never help him.

Alexander collapsed to the floor. He writhed in pain, emitting a guttural scream. His face was contorted—his thin, cracked lips curved up, exposing his teeth. He dug his nails on the floor, drawing blood.

"Stop it," she pleaded, looking at Alderic. "Leave him alone."

"Sit down," he said, gesturing to the empty chair across the table.

"You can't tell me what to do," she said, her jaw locked.

Alexander screamed again and Alderic smiled. "I'll kill him. He's not as useful as I had hoped."

Lana ran to the chair. She pulled it out so fast the leg hit her shin, sending a shockwave of pain through her. She sat down and rubbed the sore spot.

Alderic smiled. He picked up a butter knife from the place setting, twirling it in the air. Alexander finally stopped screaming. The door opened again, and Damon marched into the room, dragging Terris behind him. Lana stood, tipping her chair over.

Damon threw Terris into one of the chairs. He took a step back, glaring at Alexander who was still on the floor, breathing heavily. When he looked up again, his gaze settled on Lana's chair.

"Are you going to pick that up?" he asked.

She stared at Damon defiantly, challenging him to do something about it. Alexander writhed on the floor.

"Get him out of here," Alderic said, placing the knife back on the table.

Damon knelt next to Alexander. Lana watched with bated breath as her cousin took hold of his cloak and stood up, heaving him. Before Alexander had a chance to recover, Damon dragged him away.

When the door shut behind them, the room was eerily quiet. She looked at her friend, suppressing the urge to run to him. He looked straight ahead, toward the window.

"Are you okay?" she whispered.

He didn't answer, and she didn't need one; she knew he wasn't. His cloak was torn, and his face was dirty. His left cheek was marked with a large cut and his hands were red, the skin raw.

"Lana, sit down."

She glared at Alderic. Although she was terrified of him, she didn't want to listen to him—to blindly obey him like his rebels. She ran toward her friend. Before she reached him, she flew backward, as if two invisible hands had picked her up and flung her away.

"I asked you to sit down." Alderic slammed his hands on the table.

Terris turned to her. He pushed his chair backwards, as if he were going to stand up and walk to her, to help her. Alderic picked up the butter knife and threw it past his left ear, barely missing. It fell on the floor near Lana. Terris stopped moving, his face pale.

"Enough of this." Alderic stood up, his body towering over them. "Sit down before I do something you won't like."

Lana had no choice. She couldn't risk Terris being hurt. She brushed off her cloak before making her way to the table.

"Now, isn't this nice?" Alderic was enjoying her submission and helplessness.

Terris sniffled. Lana hoped he would look up at her. His head was down, and his eyes were trained on his hands.

"I'm really not that bad," Alderic began. "I'm afraid my brother has been feeding you all kinds of lies."

"Let him go," she interrupted. "I'll do whatever you want, as long as you let him go."

Alderic was quiet. He leaned back in his chair—his eyes locked on hers. It took everything inside of her to hold his gaze. She had to stay strong. She needed to outsmart him.

"He's holding you back," he said a moment later. "You're not friends. This bond you feel, this friendship—it's only an illusion."

She watched him, her eyes only darting away for a split second to look at Terris. Her friend looked up at Alderic. He opened his mouth, wanting to say something but was too scared.

Alderic leaned forward again, setting his hands on the table. "I linked you during the ceremony. You were supposed to die," he added, turning to Terris.

"Why?" he asked, his lips quivering. "Why would you want to kill a baby?"

"You were weak," Alderic answered matter-of-factly. "Amos practically begged me to do it. You were covered."

"Covered?" she asked, trying to understand what he was saying.

A tear slid down her friend's cheek. She wanted to get up—to comfort him, but knew Alderic wouldn't be happy. Her hands wrapped around the edge of the chair and her knuckles turned white from the pressure.

"Two weeks after you were born," he began, "Shandra delivered a baby encased in the fluid from the womb. This is a sign of weakness." He turned to look at Terris. "You were never meant for this world—you were supposed to die fifteen years ago."

"Why would you link us?" she asked.

Alderic looked up at her. "To make you strong. Because you're linked you have his magic, his power within you. Now that you're home, it's awakened. He was supposed to die but since the ceremony was interrupted, he didn't and you're still connected. You'll always be drawn to him."

She tried to comprehend what he was telling her. Terris squared his shoulders but another tear slid down his cheek, betraying his false sense of bravery. Lana's mind worked in overdrive, trying to think straight. She looked at her friend. Was it true? Were they only friends because they were linked?

"Kill him."

She inhaled sharply. He couldn't be serious. This was a new low. He couldn't expect her to kill her friend, could he?

"Lana," Alderic said, interrupting her thoughts. "He's holding you back. He's making you weak."

She shook her head. She couldn't believe what he was asking her to do. How could she kill her friend? How could he so easily talk about murder?

"I won't do it. Just let him go. I'll find the Crystal for you."

Alderic withdrew a large silver dagger from a pocket in his cloak. The shiny blade glinted from the sun pouring through the window. He looked at the dagger hungrily, excited by the thought of murder.

"If you won't do it, I will," he said. "But I should let you know it won't be quick if I do it."

Her body trembled. Terris screamed, pleading for his life to be spared. A low ringing muffled her hearing. She heard Terris talking, but couldn't actually make out what he was saying.

Alderic stood. She wondered if she could somehow teleport herself and Terris out of Medora. If she got to him first, would she even be able to do it? Her mind raced and she wished she knew how to control the magic. It seemed to come and go at the most random times.

"I'll do it."

A smile crept upon Alderic's face, giving him a childlike

appearance. He sat down and placed the dagger on the table. While looking at Lana, he slid it toward her. It came to a stop, mere inches from her. With shaking hands, she reached for the dagger, surprised at how heavy it was.

She stood up and took a step toward her friend. His eyes were wide, and he clutched the table in front of him. Her legs felt heavy, and each step was painful. She saw Alderic watching her, waiting to see if he would need to intervene.

As she made her way closer to Terris, a lump formed in her throat. She swallowed, hoping to dislodge it. The dagger seemed to weigh her down.

When she was standing before him, she took a deep breath, praying that her plan would work. Terris trembled before her, his body shaking in waves. She resisted the urge to hug him, to tell him that everything would be okay. Instead she held the dagger with both hands, poised to strike.

"That's it," Alderic urged. "Once it's done, you'll feel free. You'll no longer be connected."

Lana reached out with her left hand and placed her palm on her friend's cheek. She wanted to be sure she was touching him—his skin. She didn't know if it would make a difference— she couldn't remember if she was touching his hand or his cloak when they teleported to Medora. She closed her eyes and willed themselves somewhere, anywhere but here. She heard Alderic gasp. He had figured out what she was doing and couldn't believe her audacity.

When she reopened her eyes, she saw it hadn't worked. Alderic launched himself at them. She knew she was in trouble and Terris was as good as dead. Instinctively, she held her right arm out, willing everything to stop.

Everything froze, including Alderic. He was stuck mid-stride. The look on his face was terrifying. His eyes were narrowed. They appeared cold, devoid of life, reminding her of the wax figures of celebrities she had seen in Mt. Sinclair. Her friend's breathing was shallow, reminding her of their predicament. Terris was still waiting for the blow from the dagger.

He opened his eyes. "What happened?"

"I stopped time. I was touching you so you didn't freeze."

Lana pulled her friend up. She squeezed his hands tight before placing the dagger in his palms.

"Take it," she said. "In case this doesn't hold we'll have to fight him."

He shook his head, his eyes wide. "I can't."

She didn't respond. Instead, she gestured to the door. She didn't know where they were going to go, or how long time would be frozen. She opened the door and ran into the hall, immediately stopping when she saw Damon and Alexander.

Terris collided into her. When he saw why she had stopped, he stepped around her to go to his uncle. Both Damon and Alexander were immobile, caught in the moment. Alexander was carrying a large tray of food, while Damon walked behind him.

"Can you unfreeze him?" Terris asked, looking at Alexander. "Just him."

Lana shook her head. She didn't even know how everyone had unfroze when it happened in Bridian Square. As much as she wanted to try, she couldn't risk unfreezing everyone until they were safe.

"We have to help him," Terris said. "This isn't right."

"I don't know how long I can hold this. It may only last another minute or two."

Terris held the dagger out, studying it. She nudged him to move. He rushed to Alexander and put the dagger into his pocket. He turned back to Lana, looking past her. As much as she wanted to take the dagger with them, she knew it was the right thing to do.

They ran down the hall. She pressed Terris to go down the stairs since she already knew there wasn't a way out upstairs. Thankfully, they didn't meet anyone on the way, but it was also dark. They stumbled down the steps to a door, light sneaking out through the cracks in the door frame.

Lana placed her hand on the doorknob. She turned it, wondering what was waiting for them on the other side. It swung open to a large cave. Thin stalactites hung from the ceiling, reaching for them.

A few yards ahead, sunshine poured into the cave, a stark contrast from the darkness they had left. She heard running water and saw a large rock formation leading to a river. At the bank, about 50 yards from where they stood, were a cluster of rebels. She was surprised to see that they weren't immobile too. Although she should have known since the river was flowing. The rebels were digging into the dirt and rock. She stopped short, not wanting to be seen.

"There are rebels down there," she whispered so low she wasn't sure Terris even heard. "The spell must have broken. We have to hurry."

She pointed down the path, letting him know to follow. As she jogged toward the light, she wondered what the rebels were digging for. When they reached the end of the path her stomach sank. They were at a dead-end. The water flowed off the rocky cliff, creating a spectacular waterfall.

While the drop didn't appear too far, she didn't want to jump. Terris pointed to the edge. She knew they didn't have much of a choice. They needed to get as far away from Alderic and his rebels as soon as they could. The faster they left, the sooner they could secure help for Alexander. She bit her lip, wondering if Alderic would just pull her back to him at some point now that he knew he could do it. Terris took her hand.

"On the count of three," he said, holding her gaze. "One, two—"

He paused, squeezing her hand again.

"Three," they said together.

They stepped off the ledge. The wind whipped her hair and she closed her eyes, bracing herself for the impact. She didn't let go of her friend's hand. She held onto him as if her life depended on it—and at the moment, it did.

12

THE ESCAPE

The wind battered Lana. Her hair whipped across her face as she clung to Terris. After what seemed like hours, she landed in the icy cold water and her muscles tensed. The force of the impact pushed her deep below the surface. She opened her eyes when Terris let go of her hand. She couldn't see anything as she sank deeper. She knew if she didn't calm herself she would drown, so she reached her arms above her head and kicked her way to the surface.

The maneuver worked. She broke free and inhaled a deep mouthful of air, taking in the surroundings. She was near the waterfall, but Terris was nowhere to be seen. She frantically looked around again. When she didn't see him, she dove into the water, searching for any movement.

When she came up for air, she heard splashing and was relieved to see her friend a few feet away. She rode the current until she reached the riverbank. She pulled herself out and tried to catch her breath. Next to her, Terris got out of the water too. He collapsed on the grass.

Lana looked back at the cliff. No one had seen them, but the longer they stayed in the open, the greater the chance someone would. She removed her cloak and wrung out the excess water.

They made their way into the thick forest. She was grateful to be free, away from Alderic, but they were still in Medora. She looked at her friend, thankful that he was with her, and they had both managed to escape. They walked in silence. When the trail widened, alerting them that it was often used, they ducked into the thick underbrush.

"Do you think they're close?" Terris asked. "Where can we hide?"

"I don't know."

Lana's mind raced. Would Alderic pull her back to him? She remembered the pain in her stomach. She felt fine now— scared, but no stomach pain. Just when she thought her life was spiraling out of control, it got worse. The fact that Alderic was able to manipulate her dreams and pull her to him was terrifying.

A cold burst of wind blew around them, wrapping her in the coldest hug. Her wet clothes clung to her. She was uncomfortable and wanted to go home. She wanted to see her parents. She wanted to get as far away from Medora, and Alderic, as possible. She wanted her life to go back to normal.

"Do you think what he said is true?" Terris asked, his voice cracking. "We're linked?"

She looked behind them, making sure they weren't being followed. "I don't know. Even if it's true, it doesn't change anything. On my end at least."

"We became friends rather quickly." Terris pushed a tree branch out of their path, holding it so she could pass. "I've spent my whole life in the castle. Everyone ignored me until you came along. I feel like I've known you forever."

Her throat tightened and she swallowed, pushing the lump down into her stomach. "I won't let anything happen to you. I won't let him hurt you."

The words hung in the air, surrounding them, reminding them both of their connection. They had only met a month ago. Even though they had been through so much together in such a short amount of time, she wondered if it was normal to feel so protective of someone she just met.

Her damp clothes weighed her down as she walked. She tried clearing her head, wanting more than anything to forget that she had powers and abilities that she couldn't control. She bit her lips. They were so dry even placing them together hurt.

"I found something at Willow Manor," Terris said.

She looked up at him, waiting for him to continue. He looked straight ahead—his eyes trained on something in the distance. Their visit to Willow Manor seemed so long ago.

"I found pictures of my parents in the library," he said. "My mother and Kiernan's mother were third cousins."

"Really?" Lana was surprised to hear that they were related. "I didn't know."

Terris nodded. "I've seen my parents before."

He turned away from her. She was confused. She knew his father was in the Yards and his mom had disappeared. Had he seen his mother? If so, where? When he didn't say anything, she reached for his arm and they stopped walking.

"Where?"

"In the castle," he answered. "The figures in the hall. The dancing ones."

She gasped. She hadn't meant to, but his words had surprised her. She remembered seeing the ghostly, dancing figures and never would have guessed they were his parents. "How do you know?"

"I went to the library to look for something to read to pass the time. I was reaching for a book on the top shelf and a photo album fell. When I picked it up, a picture caught my eye. As soon as I saw them, I knew who they were. Their names were even written at the bottom—Amos and Shandra."

The hair on her arm prickled, as if speaking their names would summon them. They were horrible people, and she hoped Terris never found them.

"I had seen the apparitions so many times," he continued, his voice quivering. "I walked by them so many times."

"I'm sorry, Terris. You deserve better. You deserve so much more than them. My father is a horrible person, but at least I have my parents—my real parents." Her stomach sank. "I hope they're all right."

"I'm sure they are."

"What I'm trying to say is you're too good for them. They don't deserve you."

"You don't know what it's like to be alone—to have no one," he said. "Maybe they changed their mind? Maybe they've been painted into these terrible people and it was never true. Maybe they wanted me this whole time, and Alderic forced them into everything."

As the words flew out of his mouth, he recoiled, as if even he didn't believe them. She stepped closer to her friend. She took his hands in hers and squeezed them.

"You're not alone anymore. You have me. You're my family. You always have been. We may have been brought together through less than ideal circumstances, but we're in this together."

He looked up at her, a tear falling down his cheek. She suppressed the impulse to reach up and wipe it away. His green eyes locked on hers and for the first time she noticed how striking they were. The tiniest specks of yellow surrounded his pupils, a stark contrast to the dark-green.

A large brown bird took flight from a nearby tree, and she dropped his hands. She stepped back and he wiped the last tears from his face. They were drawn out of their conversation when she heard a sound she desperately wished she had imagined. Terris cleared his throat, oblivious, and she turned toward him. Her finger flew in front of her lips, signaling him to remain quiet.

Several strong gusts of wind blew around them, lifting the hair off her shoulders. She froze, her hands limp at her sides, as a flash of black spun around them. A sense of dread overtook her. She couldn't believe how foolish they had been. Even though they were in the dense forest, thin slivers of light found their way through the canopy of leaves.

Another gush of wind curled around her, wrapping her in its cold embrace. A large black beast appeared before her. It stood on its hind legs and sniffed the air, mere inches from her. They stood very still, too afraid to move. She remembered her first meeting with the Shadow Splinters. Queen Gwendolyn had referred to them as Alderic's beasts. She should have known they would be in Medora, near him.

The Shadow Splinter before them disappeared, in front of her one moment, the next gone in a film of thick black smoke. Terris reached for her arm, grasping it tightly. He dug his nails into her skin. Another beast appeared a few feet away. It took a slow step toward them. She held her breath as the awful sulfur smell wafted toward her.

The beast turned around and dropped on all fours. It arched its back and looked up at the sky. A moment later, it ran to their left, toward a group of three other beasts, all wearing long dark cloaks that covered their thick-brown fur.

Lana pointed to their right. She took a slow step, pausing when her foot touched the ground to make sure they hadn't been heard. When it seemed they were safe, they continued walking, staying in the shadow of the trees. Terris held her arm so tight she feared she would lose circulation, but didn't say anything for fear the beasts would hear.

Her stomach lurched when she heard them growl. The monsters were looking in their direction, sniffing the breeze. She stopped walking, holding Terris back as well. Even though the beasts were blind to everything but shadows, their other senses were stronger—including smell. Her whole body trembled, and she sucked in a mouthful of air in a feeble attempt to steady her nerves.

As she took another deep breath, black smoke surrounded them. When she inhaled, the thick air snaked down her throat. She coughed, trying to push the smoke out of her lungs. A large beast appeared in front of Terris. It was standing on its hind legs, its arms reaching for them. Terris dropped her hand and stepped backward, hitting a large tree trunk.

Lana knew it was only a matter of time before her friend was captured. Running wasn't an option. The Shadow Splinter was too close to Terris for him to escape. Her only option would be to distract it, lure it away.

Before she had a chance to move, one of the beasts let out an ear-piercing howl. She threw her hands over her ears, trying to drown out the sound. The Shadow Splinter before Terris turned around, toward the sound, before disappearing.

Terris ran to her, hugging her tightly. Her breath caught in her throat, thankful that he was all right. The beast reappeared, but they didn't waste any time to see what had drawn its attention. Lana began running. Her heart pounded in her chest as she dodged trees, the branches reaching for her.

"Something's happening," Terris panted next to her.

She turned to look at him, narrowly missing a large tree trunk. Terris had stopped running. His back was toward her, looking at the group of Shadow Splinters huddled over the fallen body of one of their own. She wasn't sure why Terris cared. This was their chance to escape—to get as far away as they could.

Then Lana saw them. They were wearing long scarlet robes. Even in the distance, she saw their blood-red lips.

"What are they doing?" Terris whispered.

The Outcasts had cornered the Shadow Splinters. They

were chanting, but she couldn't hear what they were saying. They were too far away.

"They'll help us get home. They're on our side."

Terris stumbled again, almost falling to the ground. The beasts shrieked, their cries echoing around them. A dozen birds, blue with streaks of green interwoven in their feathers, flew above them. Suddenly, blue fire surrounded the Shadow Splinters. The flames raged around their feet. They cried out, the sound piercing her ears. As one, they disappeared, a thick cloud of black smoke curled high into the air where they once stood.

"We still have time to make a run for it," Terris whispered.

As if they heard him, the Outcasts turned in their direction. Something was pulling her to them. Her legs began moving, as if on their own. Terris scrambled to catch up to her. The Outcasts were walking in unison, spread out in a line. Before she could comprehend what was happening, she was before them.

"You shouldn't be here," one of the women said. "It isn't safe."

They were still standing in a line, holding hands. They closed their eyes and began chanting. The wind picked up, blowing around them so fierce, Lana stumbled backward. The wind seemed to be centered around them. It slowed, cocooning them. The women opened their eyes.

"Quiet," one warned.

"Someone's coming," another added.

The woman closest to Lana pointed to their left. Her stomach dropped at the sight of a rebel, his long black cloak moving silently through the trees.

"He can't see us," one of the women said. "Or hear us."

Lana watched the rebel stalk past them, oblivious that he was so close to his targets. She was so nervous she thought her legs would give out. When the rebel disappeared, the women dropped each other's hands and the bubble of wind around them disappeared. She felt vulnerable, exposed. A shiver passed through her.

"We don't have much time," a woman with long glossy black hair said.

She had barely finished speaking when they turned. In their place were the monstrous beings Alderic cursed them into many years ago. Their perfect cloaks were reduced to rags. Their faces were unrecognizable, their skin was wrinkled. Their eyes were sunken into their face and they looked emaciated. Even though she had been expecting it based on her first encounter with them, she was still caught off guard. Just as quickly as they had changed, they became human again.

"We've been tracking you," the woman with the black hair continued. "Ever since the attack at Port Morgan."

"How'd you know about that?" Lana asked, trying to push the memory of the awful night behind her. "Do you know if they're all right? My family?"

The woman at the far right stepped forward. Her skin glowed, and her long curly brown hair was in a loose bun. Tiny white flowers were tucked in her hair.

"I was there," the woman said. "I'm not sure if they made it. They were ambushed. They weren't prepared."

The words hit her, sucking the life out of her. *They weren't prepared.*

"What does that mean?" Terris asked, saying the words that she couldn't.

The women transformed again. It didn't seem as if they had noticed the change, or if they did, they were so used to it that it no longer fazed them. Lana thought of her parents. What was she going to do if something happened to them? Her thoughts shifted to Ramos. How were Deliah and Dominic going to react to the news?

"I don't know," the woman answered. "Death met them in Port Morgan. How many fell, I am unsure."

Hot tears welled at Lana's eyes. Her hands flew to her mouth. She took a deep breath and felt Terris's arms around her.

"We don't know much more," the first woman said as they changed back.

A faint string of hope dangled before her, and she clung to it. They couldn't be dead. She would hold onto hope that they were alive. They were out there, searching for her. She just had to find them.

"How were you tracking us?" Terris asked. "It's odd that you appeared just in time to save us."

Lana narrowed her eyes at her friend. She didn't want to anger them. They had helped her, on more than one occasion. She didn't care how they found them. She was just thankful they came when they did.

"Your magic has a signature all its own," she said, looking at Lana. "We used it to track you."

She didn't know how to interpret that. Was it a good thing or a bad thing? Was that why Alderic was able to pull her to him so easily?

"Where's Angelica?" Lana asked, changing the subject. She didn't want to think about her magic anymore. Or the fact that it had its own signature.

"She's safe," a woman with curly red hair answered.

The Outcasts looked at each other as if sharing a secret. Their covert glances didn't escape her, and she wondered what they were hiding. She had learned of Angelica's sad past the first time she met the Outcasts. When Angelica's parents betrayed Alderic, he murdered them. He also stabbed Angelica, who had only been a few months old. The Outcasts, astonished that Alderic would go so far as to harm a baby, were able to save her by putting her spirit into her doll, which was where she had been for the past sixteen years.

"You need to leave Medora."

Lana threw her hands up in frustration. Did they think she was on vacation? Just doing a little sight-seeing in Medora? The woman with the long black hair seemed to read her irritation.

"You need to use your magic."

"I can't," she stammered. "I don't know what I'm doing."

Terris cleared his throat. "You brought us here. You can bring us back."

"No. I already told you that I don't know how. He brought me here. I didn't."

"He used your magic," the woman said. "Your abilities. He may have called you, but it originated from you. You can do it again."

"You can do it, Lana," Terris pleaded. "You can bring us back to Bridian."

She shook her head. Why wasn't anyone listening to her?

"All you have to do is believe," the woman with the curly red hair said as they changed before her eyes again.

"Can you give us the directions? We'll walk. Maybe we can find someone with a carriage," she added hopefully.

"He's looking for you," the woman with the long dark hair said. "You don't have long."

Lana sighed. "How? How does it work?"

The woman with the curly red hair stepped forward. "You simply need to believe that you can do it. It's already ingrained in you. You need to believe."

"It doesn't work that way." She crossed her arms over her chest. "Just believing isn't enough."

"You need to become someone who can teleport," the woman with the black hair said. "Someone whose magic flows through them, making them stronger. Someone that controls their power."

"That is to truly believe in yourself," the woman with the red curly hair added sagely.

Lana rolled her eyes. She hadn't meant to. It was a reflex. She closed her eyes and willed herself to teleport to the other side of Terris. When nothing happened, she reopened her eyes and sighed loudly.

"See?"

"You're scared," Terris said.

She rubbed her forehead. "Of course I am! Wouldn't you be? I have no idea what I'm doing. I don't even know how long I'll even be here," she added. "Alderic could call me back to him at any moment and I have no idea how to stop it."

"I know," he added, his voice cracking. "I'm just agreeing that it's hindering you."

"Act as if you have done it hundreds of times," one of the Outcasts said—Lana couldn't tell which one because she was still glaring at her friend. "It was you, your power that brought you to Medora. You can leave of your own accord. You just need to believe that you can do it. You did it once, you can do it again."

"The sooner we get back to Bridian, the sooner we'll be able to get help for everyone in Port Morgan," Terris said. "We can alert the army, let them know there was an attack—that King Ramos was attacked. They may not know yet."

She sucked in a deep breath. She knew that he was right. Or maybe they were already on their way back to the castle? Maybe she would see her parents sooner than she thought. Her stomach fluttered at the thought.

"The rebels will be back," one of the Outcasts said.

Lana closed her eyes. If there was one thing that would motivate her to try—to really try, it was her parents. She desperately wanted to see them.

When nothing happened, she took another breath, letting it fill her lungs. She remembered the Outcasts' advice. She had to believe that she could do it. She had to act like the version of herself that mastered teleportation. She imagined herself on the other side of Terris. She honed in on the jolt of excitement that sprouted in her belly.

Her stomach churned and she knew she was close. It was the same feeling that had begun before she had teleported to Medora. She suppressed the urge to open her eyes and stop. She didn't want the fear to overcome her, not when her parents needed her help.

The churning sensation morphed into tiny pin-pricks deep in her belly. It felt as if she was being stabbed from the inside. A dark, guttural sound escaped her lips. She gasped for breath and opened her eyes, surprised to see that she was on her hands and knees. She looked up and saw Terris next to her, on the opposite side of where he had been moments ago.

"You did it!" he exclaimed, bending down to help her stand. "I knew you could."

A wave of nausea hit her. Her head felt cloudy, as if trying to adjust to the change. While she was glad it had worked, it seemed too easy. Almost as if someone had helped her. Terris smiled, his enthusiasm radiating outward. Then it hit her.

"It's easier because I'm with you."

He narrowed his eyes, not understanding. His head tilted to the left and his smile disappeared. Everything was beginning to make sense. They were connected. She was drawing from him —his magic.

"We're connected," she whispered. "I'm drawing from you. That's why it's been so easy. That's why everything has come so easily to me."

He didn't say anything, still lost in confusion.

"Good," the woman with the long black hair acknowledged. "You are connected. Use it. Use it to defeat him—to set us free."

Lana spun toward the woman. That was the reason they had been keeping tabs on her—watching her. They had an ulterior motive. They wanted her to stop the curse. The problem was, she didn't think she would ever be strong enough to reverse it.

"It's okay," Terris whispered. "I've never been good at it—at anything. You might as well use it."

He didn't understand. She had siphoned his magic, stolen it from him. Where he struggled, she excelled. She needed to find the Crystal and put this whole mess behind her. Perhaps when the Crystal was destroyed, and Alderic was imprisoned, she would be able to break the connection.

"How do we break it?" Lana asked. "How can I give him his magic back?"

"You can't," the woman with the shiny black hair answered.

Lana didn't believe her. They wanted to be free from the curse. They were counting on her to break it. They wouldn't help her give back the magic. Not if they thought she needed it. She would have to figure out a way to give it back to Terris on her own.

She remembered the drawings and her hands flew to her pocket. She withdrew them and her heart sank. They were soaked from their escape. She carefully unfolded the papers, but they were unrecognizable.

"I found these at Poklin's." She sighed. "I know the rebels used to meet there. They were two sketches. Damon drew them."

She pictured them, trying to remember every detail. She explained them, providing as much description as she could remember. The Outcasts remained silent. She closed her eyes, picturing the second drawing. She had studied them so often she was surprised she had to think about it, that the information hadn't just sprang to mind.

When she finished, she folded the papers and slid them in her pocket. The Outcast with the long black hair shook her head. "It doesn't sound as if it's from this world."

"I figured as much," she said. "I think it's somewhere in Mt. Sinclair."

"Go now. They're close."

"It will be harder for him to pull you again," another added. "Once you learn to control it, no one will be able to."

"How do I control it? How do I make sure he doesn't pull me to him again?"

The Outcasts didn't answer. They changed before her again. They surrounded them. Up close, she saw their eyes were a pale yellow. Their skin was marked with red welts.

"More are coming," the woman with the red curly hair warned. "Go."

Lana took a deep breath and closed her eyes. She pictured Bridian. She pictured the castle. She knew without a shadow of doubt that when she reopened them, she would be home. Heat emanated from her friend's hands, and she curled her fingers within his, soaking it up, allowing his energy to flow into her. She took another deep breath and felt the ground disappear beneath her feet.

13

HOME

The first thing Lana saw was Terris. His eyes were shut tight, creases lining his outer lids. She dropped his hands, and he opened his eyes. He looked around the room.

"You did it," he said. "You really did it!"

He wrapped his arms around her tightly. Her heart hammered in her chest, the adrenaline making her dizzy. She looked around the room in awe. It worked. She had brought them to Bridian. They were safe in her room at the castle.

"I told you that you could do it," Terris added.

Lana's skin tingled. She felt light, as if she was floating. She walked to the trunk at the foot of her bed and ran her hands along it, feeling the textured wood. Everything looked just as she had left it, except the bed had been made. The familiar tick of the grandfather clock drew her attention and she spun around to face it. She watched the pendulum gracefully glide from side-to-side, still in awe of her abilities.

"Do you think they're back?" Terris asked hopefully. "Your parents? King Ramos?"

In her excitement, she had momentarily forgotten about

them. She immediately came back to reality. She ran to her door and was greeted by an empty hallway.

"It's strange to not see Grant here."

Lana hoped that he was all right. While she didn't like the constant supervision, she would never wish anything bad happen to him.

"They still might be here," Terris said. "No one knows we're back yet. Grant wouldn't be sitting outside an empty room."

He was right. Her heart fluttered, not ready to give up hope. She ran down the hall. When they reached the main staircase, she flew down the steps so fast it hardly felt as if her feet touched them.

The foyer was empty. She stopped at the bottom of the stairs and looked toward the dining hall. She was surprised to see it was empty. Usually, soldiers patrolled the foyer.

It was so quiet, their footsteps echoed. Terris walked past her to the hall. He returned after scouting the place.

"Empty."

"I don't understand." She crossed her arms. "Where is everyone?"

Something felt off; she was reminded of the night they found the Crystal. The castle had been eerily quiet then too. If only she had known the darkness that had been following them. Was it a sign? A warning?

Before her thoughts had a chance to overtake her, she saw Damarius walking briskly toward them. When he saw them, he stopped. His hand flew to his chest as if he couldn't believe what he was seeing.

"Princess Lana," he said, bowing. "How did you get here? Where have you been?"

"Where are my parents?" she asked, the words spilling out of her. "Where is everyone?"

In response, Damarius looked to the ground. He didn't have to say anything. They weren't here.

"Where is everyone?" she repeated, her voice cracking.

Damarius sighed. "Late last night we got word of the attack at Port Morgan. One of our soldiers escaped and rode straight here."

"Is everyone all right?"

"King Ramos is alive. We're unsure of the others."

Lana felt the life drain from her. Like a popped balloon, everything rushed out of her, deflating her.

"We sent our extra soldiers to Port Morgan," he continued. "The ones we could spare anyway. From what I was told, only a few perished."

Only a few perished. The words assaulted her. They made her sick as they struck deep within her belly. Out of everything that she had been through the last month, who would have guessed four little words would be her undoing.

She turned her back to him, trying to hide the tears that poured out of her. They came in a flood, every memory spilling out. Terris ran to her side as she collapsed.

"We don't know anything else," Damarius said. "King Ramos will be here soon. I'm sure your parents will be with him."

She wiped her face, trying to clear her head. She knew she shouldn't worry yet—that there was no use crying over something that may not even be true. Her parents, and Grant, may still be alive. There was no use expending the energy, living in the darkness now.

Terris helped her stand. She brushed off the despair and turned to Damarius.

"Please let me know if you hear anything else."

She didn't wait for an answer. She turned on her heel and walked to the staircase, leaving Terris behind. She needed to be alone.

She ran up the stairs, taking them two at a time and made a beeline for her room. All she wanted to do was take a shower and sleep until her parents were home. She closed the door behind her.

Lana stepped up to the mirror above her dresser. She looked at her reflection, searching deep within the glass. Her face was dirty, and her hair was tangled. Deep bags lined her eyes, and her face was pale. She turned away. She opened the top drawer of the dresser and pulled out clean clothes, slamming the drawer closed.

The mirror caught her attention again and she found herself watching the stranger in front of her, wondering if life would ever feel normal again. She bit her lip as anger boiled inside her. Now that she was safe, it felt as if her emotions were overtaking her. She marched to the bathroom and turned on the shower, letting the steam fill the room. She felt lighter afterwards.

Despite the absence of normalcy in the castle, one thing didn't fail to function—her food had been delivered to her room. She lifted the lid and inhaled the comforting aroma of the creamy soup. Her stomach rumbled and she brought the tureen to her bed and sat. After she ate, she placed the dishes in the hall. She fell asleep before her head hit the pillow, more than happy to put the past few days behind her.

When she awoke, she remembered the nightmares that had tormented her throughout the night. Visions of Alderic and Contlay swirled through her head, reminding her that she had to find the Crystal. She knew that once it was recovered, everything would settle—her life would return to normal.

She was greeted by the empty hallway once again. She ignored Grant's absence, not wanting to fall down the emotional spiral and made her way downstairs. She hoped there was news of her parents. When she stepped into the dining hall, she was taken aback by how empty it was. It shouldn't have come as a surprise, but it was still a shock and a reminder that her loved ones may never return.

Her cousins were sitting at their usual seats and her Aunt Charlotte was at the head of the table, buttering a piece of toast. Marnie and her parents were sitting at the far table next to Nick and his mother. Besides that, the room was empty. Deliah looked up.

"We've been so worried about you," she said. "Terris told us everything that happened last night. I went to see you but you were already asleep."

Lana embraced her cousin fondly. "How are you. How are things here?"

Charlotte cleared her throat. "Deliah, let Lana sit."

Dominic looked up from his plate, nodding to her. A few minutes later, Terris walked into the room. He was holding a silver tray, which he placed in front of Charlotte, who only waved him away.

The silence was unnerving. Lana was used to the dining hall full of people, bursting with life. She spread her napkin on her lap, trying to avoid looking at the two empty chairs on either side of her. A lump formed in her throat and she took a sip of the water in front of her.

"I was informed of your return last night," Charlotte said, setting her toast down. "I felt it wise to let you rest."

"Thank you," Lana said. "Has there been any news? About my parents?"

Charlotte shook her head, finally meeting Lana's gaze. "No."

A quiet sob escaped Deliah's lips. Dominic took his sister's hand. "Dad's fine, Del," he said. "Everyone's fine."

Lana reached for her tea. Her hand trembled as she brought the cup to her lips and drank, focusing on the warm liquid sliding down her throat rather than letting her thoughts overwhelm her. The room was too quiet. No one spoke.

Dominic pushed his plate away and pulled out a small notebook and pencil. He lightly drew the pencil over the paper, sketching the food on the table. Lana watched him for a moment, lost in thought. There were only two people who could have taken the Crystal, besides herself and Terris. Alderic already confirmed he didn't have it. That meant Contlay did.

She didn't think the papers she found in Poklin's were of someplace in Bridian, or Telorian. She had a suspicion they were someplace in Mt. Sinclair. The paper reminded her of printer paper from her former life. She already deduced that Damon had made the drawings. She knew he visited Mt. Sinclair once, had even met with Contlay. He had introduced him to the Rebellion.

Across the room, Nick pushed his chair back loudly. Lana froze. She didn't know what the drawings were, but maybe he would.

"Dominic, can I borrow your pencil, and a piece of paper?"

He tore a sheet of paper from his notebook. He slid the paper and the pencil toward her. Lana drew the sketches from memory. When she finished, she took one last sip of tea and stood. She caught Terris's eye from across the room and gestured to the hall. He nodded subtly.

"Please let me know if you hear anything," Lana said to Charlotte.

The Queen brought her napkin to her lips, dabbing them. "I will."

The hall was just as quiet as she found it last night. She leaned against the wall, waiting for Nick to leave. A moment later, Deliah and Dominic joined her.

"It's too quiet out here," Deliah said, her eyes drifting to the doors, as if waiting for her father.

"What were you drawing?" Dominic asked.

Before she could answer, Nick walked out of the dining hall, flanked by his mother.

"Nick," Lana called, her voice raised. "Can I talk to you?"

"That would be nice," Mrs. Jacobs said. "Right, Nick. You've been so lonely."

He narrowed his eyes. "Make it quick."

Lana shifted on her feet, thinking of an excuse to leave Mrs. Jacobs. She wanted to ask him in private.

"Can we go upstairs?" she asked. "There's a room on the third floor where we hang out," she added, pointing to her cousins.

When Nick didn't say anything, Mrs. Jacobs smiled. "Have fun, sweetie. Go on."

Nick rolled his eyes but made his way to the stairs. Lana took that as his agreement and followed. When they came to the second floor Mrs. Jacobs waved before leaving them.

They continued in silence to the room on the third floor. Lana used the time to think of the best way to ask Nick about the papers. The possibility that the mystery may soon be solved invigorated her.

Terris was waiting for them. He was sitting on the couch. When he heard them, he looked up expectantly, wondering what Lana had wanted to talk to him about.

"I figured you would come here," he said, standing up.

Deliah waltzed to the couch and sat down. She crossed her legs underneath her, placed her elbows on her knees and her head on her hands. Dominic sat on a chair near the window, away from his sister. Nick leaned against the doorframe, clearly not wanting to stay any longer than necessary.

Lana reached into her pocket and withdrew the paper. She held it out to Nick and he grudgingly stepped forward. She placed the paper in his hands.

"Does this layout look familiar to you? Does it look like a building from Mt. Sinclair?"

Nick looked up. "Seriously? This is what you wanted to talk about? A drawing?"

"Never mind," she said, taking the paper back.

"Let me see it again," Nick said.

Lana handed him the paper. His eyes darted across it,

taking it all in. Deliah and Dominic were talking, and she suppressed the urge to shush them. Weren't they excited? Didn't they realize the mystery may about to be solved?

Nick looked up. "I do recognize it but you need to do something for me. Once you help me, I'll tell you. I'll even bring you there myself."

Lana sighed loudly. "What do you want?"

"This is in Mt. Sinclair. I'll tell you where it is when you take me with you. I want to go home."

Her mouth dropped. She didn't think she heard him right.

"You want me to bring you to Mt. Sinclair? How do you know that's something I can do?"

"You've gone back before. I've heard you can teleport."

"I told you that in confidence!" Deliah shouted.

Lana looked at her cousin. "How did you know about that?"

"He told me last night," Deliah answered, pointing to Terris. "I may have told Nick after."

"I don't know if I can teleport through dimensions," Lana said, exasperated at how fast gossip traveled around the castle corridors.

"That's my deal," he said, shrugging his shoulders. "If you bring me back, I'll even personally escort you where you need to go."

Lana tried to think of a way to bring herself and Nick to Mt. Sinclair. She remembered the mirror that led to Altaris from Nick's house, but didn't want to go anywhere near the underwater city. If the Altarians managed to capture her again they would immediately kill her.

For a moment, she thought of trying to teleport to Mt. Sinclair, but wasn't sure she wanted to take the chance. If something happened, she would never forgive herself. Lana wasn't even sure she would be able to teleport across dimensions either.

As if reading her mind, Deliah pointed to her brother. "You can try with us first."

"What?" Dominic said incredulously. "Why are you volunteering us? What if something happens? She doesn't know what she's doing."

"You can try with me," Nick said. "I'm not scared. I just want to go home. I hate it here."

"Why do you hate it here?" Deliah asked, obviously offended.

"It's not home," he answered. "I miss my dad. I miss my friends."

Lana rolled her eyes. Nick was making her so angry she didn't even feel bad for him. In fact, she wished she would be able to bring him back to Mt. Sinclair. She hoped he would stay there for good, and she would never have to see him again.

"Let's go then," Deliah said. "I'm ready."

"You want me to try now?" Lana asked, turning to her cousin.

"Yeah, why not?" Deliah asked, shrugging. "The sooner we try the better. As far as we know the demons haven't been released yet. If the place looks promising, we'll let Dad know when he gets back."

"We can't go now," she protested.

"Why?" Deliah asked.

"Well, for one thing, Nick hasn't said goodbye to his mom."

"I don't have anything to say to her," he said. "I didn't want to leave Mt. Sinclair in the first place, but she made me."

"There's nothing you want to take with you?"

Nick shook his head. Lana looked around the room and saw that everyone was watching her, waiting for her decision.

"What if I can't do it?" she asked. "What if we end up somewhere else?"

"You can do it." Deliah waved her off. "Come on, at least try. If we end up somewhere else, you can bring us back."

"That's what I'm trying to say." She was getting exasperated. She needed everyone to listen. "What if I can't bring us back? Don't you get it? I could get all of us stuck in some dimension without anyone knowing where we are."

"Then we'll figure it out," Deliah said, not understanding her concern. "Why worry about that now?"

"Come on, Laughs," Nick interrupted. "You know you want to get rid of me. Just give it a shot."

Lana thought about what they were saying. If they were caught leaving the castle without a guard she would be in a lot of trouble, but Ramos, her parents, and even Grant weren't there to stop her. She had barely escaped Alderic and knew he would try again. She had to get more comfortable teleporting. She had to practice so she could block him. All she wanted to do was check out the building that Damon had sketched.

She bit her lip, all the different possibilities swirling in her head. She wondered if going to Mt. Sinclair was a good idea and then remembered that if the demons were released, death and destruction would follow. The rebels wouldn't stop with Bridian, they would wreak havoc in every dimension. She had to do something.

"I'm probably going to regret this," she said, facing her cousins. "I can't take everyone. I'm not even going to try. I think you two should stay here."

"No!" Deliah cried.

"Why can't you take us?" Dominic asked.

"I don't have much experience. I would feel more comfortable if there were less of us."

"Come on," Deliah whined.

"I need you two to stay here," she repeated. "If we're not back in an hour, find Damarius and tell him where we went. How long does it take to get to Altaris from here on horseback?"

Dominic tilted his head in thought "About an hour and a half."

"If we aren't back in an hour, tell him where we went. Tell him to go to Altaris. One of the houses there has a mirror to Mt. Sinclair, you'll come out at Nick's house."

"That's a great plan and all, but we don't know where you're going in Mt. Sinclair," Dominic said. "You don't even know where you're going."

Her cousin was right. Nick wasn't going to tell her what the drawings were until she brought him to Mt. Sinclair.

"Will you tell Deliah and Dominic before we leave?" Terris asked.

Nick looked at Lana, trying to gauge if he could trust her to hold up her end of the bargain.

She crossed her arms over her chest. "I won't take you unless you tell them."

"Fine," he agreed.

Lana turned to Terris. She needed him to come with her. She needed his presence—his magic. Everything was easier with him.

"You'll come with me?"

He stepped closer to her. "Of course. Whatever you need."

Her heart rate increased. She had goosebumps and wasn't sure why. Maybe it was the possibility that the mystery of the drawings was about to be revealed. Even though she was nervous, she was a little thrilled to see if she could teleport to Mt. Sinclair.

"Nick, tell them what the drawings are," she said. "If we're doing this, we need to leave now."

He walked to the corner of the room and waited for Deliah and Dominic to join him. He leaned into Dominic's ear and then Deliah's ear and whispered the location to them.

"Are we good?" she asked her cousins.

"I guess," Dominic said. "Maybe we should come with you. You may need our help."

"I do need your help. I need someone to tell Damarius and he will only listen to the Prince and Princess of Bridian."

"Just go." Deliah sighed. "We'll stay here."

Lana looked at Nick, who was still across the room, and said, "You have to hold my hand."

"Oh, it gets even better," he said.

She took a deep breath. They formed a triangle standing at a 60-degree angle to each other, holding hands.

She closed her eyes, aware that everyone was watching her, and tried to concentrate. She thought of Mt. Sinclair. She would need to narrow her vision to one specific place. She thought of all the places she was familiar with and settled on her house, more specifically her bedroom. She knew that it would be the last place the rebels would be as the Bureau had been keeping tabs on it.

She pictured the bed, pushed against the far wall facing the window. She imagined her desk where she used to do her homework and her closet, random magazine articles taped on the door. She even pictured the mirror that used to be a portal to Bridian, until Ramos broke the connecting mirror when they had escaped.

Lana felt the familiar tug in her stomach and braced herself for the pull. She wondered what she was going to do if they didn't end up in Mt. Sinclair, before realizing that it was too late to worry. She pushed another image of her bedroom into her mind.

When she opened her eyes, she couldn't believe what she saw. She was in Mt. Sinclair, better yet, she was in her bedroom. As Nick dropped to his knees, she shouted in glee. She couldn't believe she had done it. She felt a renewed sense of strength as she looked around the room.

The glint of glass caught her eye and she went to the mirror, remembering the last time she had seen it. She involuntarily shivered at the memory.

"Lana, you did it," Terris whispered.

She smiled and walked to the window, moving the curtains aside to reveal a sunny day. She glanced around the room once more, searching for anything she may want to bring back to Bridian with her, but didn't see anything of importance that had been missed.

They made their way downstairs, Lana leading the way. She didn't think that anyone would be in the house, but wanted to be safe just in case. When they reached the first floor, she saw that someone had picked up. New windows had been installed and the broken glass had been swept away. It even looked like someone had mopped and dusted.

She proceeded to the back door, deciding it would be easier to slip out unnoticed than the front. When she stepped into the backyard, she was surprised at how warm it was for a spring day in Mt. Sinclair. As soon as they were outside, Nick left for his house next door. He crossed the yard, without even a goodbye.

"Are you going to hold up your end of the deal?" she called, putting her hands on her hips.

"I want to see if my dad's here first," he said. "If he's not, I don't want to be stuck here alone."

Lana watched Nick make his way to his house. She should have known he would try to pull something on her and felt stupid for having trusted him in the first place. They had probably wasted a good ten minutes. The sooner they were able to get the information from Nick, the more time they would have to check out the location from the drawings.

Nick's house appeared empty. He tried to open the front door, pushing on it. When it didn't budge, he knocked but no one answered. He looked through the window.

When it became apparent that no one was inside, he swung

his foot out and kicked the door. He lost his balance and stumbled backward, colliding into Terris.

"I brought you back, Nick," Lana said. "I held up my end of the bargain. It's not my fault that your dad's not home. You need to fulfill your end. Tell us what the drawings are."

"I'll bring you there," he said. "But you have to promise that we'll check to see if my dad's home after. If he isn't, you have to bring me back."

She wasn't in the mood to argue. Even though it hadn't been a part of the original plan, she agreed to bring him back because, unlike Nick, she didn't have a mean bone in her body. She couldn't leave him stranded in Mt. Sinclair. She stepped off the porch and crossed her arms, waiting for him to lead the way when she heard a familiar voice call her name. Trevor was running to them.

Nick sighed. "Lovely."

"What are you doing here?" Trevor asked.

"It's a long story," she said, shooting Nick a warning look when he snorted. "What are you doing here?"

"I had Tech Club," Trevor answered. "My mom's working, so I'm taking the long way home."

"It's so good to see you!" Lana said, thankful at the chance to see him.

"Are you back for good?" he asked excitedly.

"No. A lot's happened. Walk with us and I'll fill you in?"

He smiled. "Where are you going? Where are your parents?"

"I don't even know where we're going," she said, gesturing to Nick. "He won't tell us."

Nick led the way as Lana told Trevor about the drawings, the attack in Port Morgan, Medora, and what they were doing in Mt. Sinclair.

"That's really scary, Lana," Trevor said.

Lana felt another lump form in her throat. She just wanted

to forget about her problems but rehashing them kept them front and center.

"How's Ava?"

"She's good," Trevor answered. "She's going to be mad she missed you."

Nick led them across the street into Frazier Woods. Lana stopped walking.

"We're going in there?" she asked, remembering when she had been attacked by rebels. "Where are we going, Nick?"

"You'll see," he called over his shoulder, enjoying the fact that she didn't know where he was taking her.

She knew they were running out of time and hoped that they would get a chance to check out wherever Nick was leading them.

"Come on," he called out when he realized they weren't following. "We're almost there. We just have to get through the woods."

Lana slowly began walking again, trying to think of where he was taking them. From their path she knew they would end up on Main Street, near the intersection of Portobello Drive. She desperately hoped he wasn't taking them to 13 Portobello Drive. The creepy house had always terrified her, and she didn't think she would be able to go in.

She tripped on an overgrown tree root and fell to the muddy grass. Someone bent down to help her stand and she was surprised to see Nick. She wondered if she should trust him and hoped he wasn't going to pretend to help her stand only to push her back down again. She took his hand.

"Thank you," she said once she was standing, wiping the mud off her cloak.

He didn't say anything. Instead, he began walking again and she looked at Trevor, her eyebrows raised in question. She knew that he found Nick's helpfulness just as puzzling as she did.

When they finally stepped out of Frazier Woods onto Main Street, Lana recalled the last time she had been there. She followed Nick down the sidewalk to Portobello Drive. Her palms began sweating as he led them across the street near the intersection.

Lana was about to tell Nick to stop walking, that she had changed her mind when he picked up his pace and walked by the old house. She breathed a sigh of relief and jogged after him, wondering where else he could be taking them when it hit her—they were going to the Mt. Sinclair Welcome Center.

14

THE STAIRCASE

Lana couldn't believe that she hadn't recognized the drawing earlier. She could clearly see the similarities now. The first drawing, which had the large box labeled *desk* was the first floor of the Welcome Center. While she wasn't sure what the second drawing represented, or how it fit with the Center, she knew it was important.

Nick climbed the stairs and paused at the door, waiting for them to catch up. When they joined him, Lana took a deep breath and opened the door. She stepped into the room, surprised that it was empty. A large desk was across the right wall, which held stacks of pamphlets touting attractions in and around Mt. Sinclair. She leafed through them, but didn't see anything out of the ordinary.

She turned from the desk, taking another look around the room. All she saw were the doors leading to the restrooms. Why had Damon taken the time to sketch the building? She knew there had to be a reason, some significance. She spun in a circle, searching for anything she may have missed.

"What are we looking for?" Trevor asked.

"I'm not sure," she said and turned to Nick. "Did you recognize the other drawing too?"

He shook his head. "I just recognized the first one. It's clearly this room. I spent too many summers volunteering here with my mom."

The mystery was eating away at her. She wanted answers, to figure out the importance of the room. She reached into the pocket of her cloak, withdrew her sketches, and unfolded them on the desk.

Pointing to the first drawing, Terris said, "The little squares are the chairs."

Everyone remained silent while they looked at the second drawing. Lana could almost hear the tick of a clock, urging her to hurry, knowing her hour was closing in. She wanted to give up out of sheer frustration.

"Why do you think the women's bathroom is circled?" Trevor asked, pointing to the circle on the first drawing.

She looked at the sketch again—he was right. She glanced at the real restroom doors, surprised to see a smaller inconspicuous door next to them. It was narrow and painted the same beige color of the room, so it had been easy to miss. She studied the sketch again and realized that the small, narrow door was the door circled in the drawings. Damon had only sketched one door for both restrooms.

Excited, she sprinted to the door and turned the handle, disappointed when she found it locked. "Well, it was worth a try."

Nick bent down at the desk, running his hand along the right side near the wall. When he stood back up, he had a key attached to a long green string in his outstretched hand.

"There's nothing in there," he said. "It's just a closet."

"How did you know that key was there?" she asked.

"My mom signed us up to volunteer here every summer. It

was so boring. I used to help Drew, or Contlay, whatever his name is, clean."

"He used to work here too?"

He nodded. "There's nothing in there though. I've been inside plenty of times."

Nick inserted the key into the lock. Lana watched with bated breath as he turned the key smoothly, unlocking the door. She stepped closer and peered into the tiny closet, disappointed that he had been right. A broom, dustpan, mop, and a bucket full of various cleaning supplies and garbage bags lined the floor.

Terris and Trevor took turns to examine the closet too. She was disappointed their trip had been in vain. She wondered how her cousins were holding up and hoped that no one had discovered her disappearance yet.

"There's a light coming from the corner," Terris said.

She was quick to get back into the closet, trying to see what Terris had found while Nick and Trevor fumbled with something in the back. Behind the bucket, a sliver of light poked through the darkness. Nick pressed up against the wall, seeing if it would move. Terris joined Nick at the back, the combined force working to let the wall up, revealing a staircase.

Lana's heart beat faster. Was Contlay up there? If so, that meant the Crystal could be up there too. Was this her chance to destroy it?

"I'm going up. Stay here."

"I'm going with you," Terris said.

"No." She shook her head. "I don't want anything to happen to any of you."

She cared about them too much. Even though she didn't like Nick, she would still feel bad if something happened to him. She crossed her arms in defiance and narrowed her eyes in a challenge.

When Terris didn't seem to be intimidated by her stance,

she said, "What are you going to do if there are rebels up there? This is my fault, not yours. This is my problem to fix."

"That's exactly why I'm going with you," Terris said, pushing his way past her. "You're not facing them alone."

"Stay here," she told Trevor and Nick, giving up on Terris.

Terris was waiting for her on the landing in between floors. He watched her climb the stairs.

When she joined him, she held him back. "Are you sure you want to come?"

He nodded. She took another deep breath and acquiesced, trying to steady her nerves. Before moving on, Terris craned his neck, trying to see what was awaiting them.

"What do you see?"

"Another room. I don't think anyone is up here."

Lana tentatively took another step. She was so nervous that something bad was going to happen she couldn't think straight. She wanted to tell Terris that she had made a mistake and they should go home, but it was too late. She looked up just in time to see him step off the staircase. He surveyed the room as she carefully made her way up the remaining steps.

They entered a large room on the second floor, although it wasn't as big as the one they had left below. There was a large desk to her left, just like the one on the first floor. A silver laptop and stacks of paper were haphazardly strewn on the surface as if they were left in a hurry. To her right was a door. This was Damon's second drawing.

Why had the room been hidden in the first place? It didn't appear as if anything of importance was there. She searched for any clues, anything that would explain why the staircase to the second floor had been concealed. She opened the laptop and shut it back in frustration when she saw it was password protected. She gently thumbed through the stack of papers, but nothing caught her eye as suspicious. The papers looked like expense reports—various numbers lined the pages.

She twirled her ring around her finger, pondering what to do next when she remembered the door. Terris seemed to read her mind. They tip-toed across the room, trying to be as quiet as possible. Lana put her ear against the wood, listening for movement on the other side.

"All clear," she said.

The door opened to a sound that both excited and terrified her. She had to cover her ears from the demons' harsh wailing. She was momentarily paralyzed as she recalled her last encounter with the Crystal. She heard the demons' cries then too. She didn't want to miss her chance to destroy it once and for all.

The room was smaller than the one they had left and was packed with furniture. Two sofas, three recliners, and a loveseat took up the majority of the space. Numerous cardboard boxes were piled among the furniture.

She took another step into the room. She heard Terris behind her and tried to ignore the demons' cries, but they were too loud. She kept her hands clasped over her ears and tried to gauge where the wailing was the loudest. She peeped behind the loveseat as it hid an entire square of area but was disappointed when she saw the space was empty.

As Lana stepped away from the loveseat, the wailing stopped. She sighed with relief and removed her hands from her ears. She glanced at Terris to make sure he was all right and saw him looking at her strangely.

"Are you okay?" he asked. "Why were you holding your hands over your ears?"

"You didn't hear them?"

"Hear who?"

"I heard them," Lana said, her eyes darting around the room. "The demons, they were so loud."

"Does that mean the Crystal's here?"

"It has to be. I heard them the last time I was near it. It has to be somewhere in this room. The demons are the loudest here."

"That means..." Terris began.

Lana looked at him. "This is Contlay's stuff. There were only two people that could have taken the Crystal. We know Alderic doesn't have it."

"What is this place?" Terris asked. "Is this where he lived?"

"I have no idea. I just hope he doesn't come back anytime soon."

She walked to a pile of boxes and scrutinized the first. She found a stack of neatly folded clothes, sweaters and jeans, and moved to another box. She was running out of time and would have to leave soon, but was so close to the Crystal she couldn't give up yet.

She heard a thud and twisted around to make sure Terris was all right. He was across the room, near the door, setting the boxes he had already looked through on the floor so he could go through those at the bottom.

After a few more minutes of searching and finding nothing but clothes, a few pieces of jewelry, and meaningless papers, Lana knew they had to leave. She had only given herself an hour. Her cousins would be worried.

"We should go." She was disappointed but knew the best thing to do was to leave. She would tell her uncle about the room so he could send someone to look for the Crystal.

She had barely made it to the door when she heard them again. They were no longer wailing. Instead, they were calling her name. She followed the sound to the far wall, to the large couch. They were so loud chills ran down her spine. She pulled the couch forward. Terris joined her at the other side and helped.

When the couch had been moved a small door had been uncovered. Without thinking, Lana opened the door. As it creaked open, a small storage room greeted her. She saw an old trunk, like the one at the foot of her bed in Bridian. How had it wound up in Mt. Sinclair?

She could feel the presence of the Crystal, she knew it was inside. She placed her hands on the lid, hoping that it was unlocked, and pushed. She was surprised when the lid opened easily, revealing the Crystal nestled securely in a red velvet blanket.

Terris was mesmerized, admiring the Crystal in awe. Lana didn't share in his amazement, knowing how troublesome her life had become because of its existence. She reached into the trunk and gingerly removed it. The demons began their verbal assault again. She tried to ignore their wailing as she held it to her chest and stood.

"Let's go."

Terris was quick to agree and made his way to the exit. Lana was still unable to accept that victory had come so easily. She couldn't wait to get back to Bridian so Ramos could help her destroy it. As she carefully traversed the path to the stairs, the Crystal let off a bright red light. The demons called her name again and she nearly dropped it.

The voices made her spine tingle. She was a few steps behind Terris when numerous black swirling shapes surrounded her, circling her and the Crystal. She was so startled she almost missed the step and nearly tumbled down the stairs. She caught her balance as one of the swirling masses flew inches from her face, leaving a cold chill in the air.

She clutched the Crystal tighter against her chest. Just as fast as the black swirling masses appeared, they disappeared. The room was quiet again and she surveyed the area, expecting them to reappear when Terris gasped.

He was on the landing between the first and second floor. She rushed to see what had startled him. Terris spun around and ran up the stairs, pushing her back to the second floor.

"What's wrong?"

Trevor and Nick were not far behind, their hands above their heads, their expressions betraying fear. A woman was hot on their tails. She had short chin-length blonde hair, green eyes and was wearing jeans and a white sweater. When she stepped off the last stair, Lana spotted the gun trained on her friends.

"I always forget to check that the panel is secure when I leave," the woman said, taking another step into the room.

She walked in a circle, looking at everyone. She paused when she saw Lana.

"Carlecia Morgan," she smiled, pointing the gun at her. "Or is it Lana Laughlin?" When Lana didn't answer, the woman continued, "I don't know what name you're going by now, nor do I care. I see you've come to release them for us."

Lana's mind raced as she tried to think of a plan to get her friends to safety. The stranger surveyed the party again, as if assessing the danger they posed. When her gaze fell upon Terris, her eyes widened in surprise.

"What's your name?" she asked, pointing the gun at him.

"Leave him alone," Lana said. "Just let them go. I'll do what you want if you let them go."

"Shut up," the woman said, still looking at him. "What's your name?"

"Terris," he said, his voice cracking. "Who are you?"

The woman laughed. She stepped closer to him. She put her forefinger under his chin, forcing him to look at her. Her next words threw out any other thought Lana had.

"My name's Shandra VanDriesen. I'm your mother."

15

THE CRYSTAL OF MEDORA

Lana was so shocked she almost dropped the Crystal. She repositioned her hands to get a better grip on it and glanced at Terris. He looked so pale she thought he was going to pass out.

"You can't be. My mother disappeared a long time ago."

"Fifteen years to be exact," Shandra said with a nod. "I've been undercover at the Bureau, biding my time until our Rebellion was stronger."

"This is the Bureau?" Lana asked, looking around the room in disbelief. "Where is everyone?"

When she had first heard of the Bureau, she had imagined a much larger operation, with a bigger office and more employees. She couldn't believe this small room was the top-secret branch of the federal government that was in contact with other dimensions. It didn't seem possible. How had Shandra, a rebel, become a part of the Bureau?

Shandra snorted. "This is only a small extension. Contlay pulled a lot of strings to have me stationed here."

"Contlay had you placed with the Bureau?" she repeated

incredulously. "How did he do that? Doesn't everyone know you're a rebel?"

Shandra tilted her head to the side. After a moment of silence, she approached Lana, Terris stood forgotten.

She tapped the gun on her left palm as she walked in a tiny circle, her eyes on Lana the whole time. "I didn't always look like this. I changed my hair, lost some weight, and began dressing differently. I took someone else's identity. Of course, I had to kill her first, along with her family, and then it was easy. The Bureau hasn't set foot in Mt. Sinclair in years. Their representatives wouldn't have recognized me even if I hadn't changed my appearance, but Contlay insisted."

"You killed someone?" Trevor's eyes were wide.

"Of course. Many someone's in fact. Comes with the territory." Her eyes lacked any remorse.

Lana felt sorry for Terris. "Let them go," she said. "They have nothing to do with this. I'll do what you want as long as you let them go."

"I don't think so." Shandra clicked her tongue. "Contlay should be back soon. I'll let him decide what to do with them."

Shandra walked over to a chair, the movement deliberate and calculated. She twirled the gun around her forefinger. She proceeded to sit down and cross her legs, displaying thin black stiletto heels.

The woman looked so different from the dancing figure in the castle. Lana studied her friend's countenance—face ashen and eyes watery—he was struggling to hold back tears.

"Why didn't you ever come for me?" he said. "Don't you care about me? Don't you love me?"

"I was never meant to be a mother," Shandra said, uncrossing her legs and standing up again. "But I don't feel like talking anymore."

"What else should we do?" Lana asked.

Shandra glared at her icily. "You need to release the demons."

"You sound like Alderic," she said, her voice gaining strength. "Whose side are you even on, his or Contlay's?"

After a long pause, Shandra answered, "The stronger side."

As she watched Shandra, an idea popped into her head. She knew her hour was probably past its limit but if she could stall, her cousins would tell Damarius where she went, and he would rescue them. She thanked her stars that Nick had told her cousins where they were going. She just needed to keep everyone alive until help arrived.

"If I release them, you think you can control them?"

Shandra's eyes lit up. "I know we can."

Lana fiddled with her feet, trying to think of something to keep her talking. Trevor and Nick were like statues near the door, both with wide eyes, taking everything in. When she looked at Terris, she felt a warmth radiate from the Crystal and nearly dropped it again. She wondered how long she would be able to hold it; she knew the demons inside were very power-ful. She struggled to think of something to keep Shandra occu-pied and hoped that her cousins already told Damarius where they were. She knew it would take him a few hours to travel to the mirror in Altaris, but it was her only hope and she clung to it.

"So, you live here?" Lana asked. "In these two rooms?"

Shandra smiled, as if remembering something funny. "I had a house. It was a nice big house left to me by some very nice acquaintances."

"Why would an acquaintance leave...oh...you killed them?"

"Like I said, it was a nice house," she said with a negligent shrug. "It was just around the corner, prime real estate."

Lana's stomach curled into a tight knot at hearing about her murderous escapades. She brushed it off and concentrated on the task in front of her.

"Are you talking about the house on Portobello Drive? Did you kill the old couple that lived there?"

"After I had them sign over the deed."

Lana wished she could have had this conversation without Terris in the room. If she was finding it difficult to stomach Shandra's ruthlessness, Terris would surely be suffering even more.

"Why are all these boxes here?" Lana asked, changing the topic and praying Shandra would take the bait. "If the house is so nice, why is all your stuff here?"

"I got tired of all the break-ins." She shrugged. "Too many people trying to sneak in to see the ghosts of the pathetic couple. For some reason everyone thought the house was haunted. Probably because I was only there at night since I was too busy keeping tabs on you during the day."

"That's right," Lana said as it all became clear. "You're the mole in the Bureau. You haven't been working with Alderic. You've been working with Contlay. He's been forming his own rebellion in Mt. Sinclair, you're helping him."

Shandra swiveled to look at her, her eyes narrowing malevolently. She took a slow step toward her. The Crystal burned Lana's hands again. She cried out in pain as the demons shrieked. She closed her eyes and tried to focus her energy on the Crystal, surprised when it began to cool. She opened her eyes to the gun pointed at her. Shandra bridged the remaining gap between them.

"When Amos and Alderic were imprisoned, I had no one," Shandra said, her mouth tight. "I was alone. I was on the run from the Council. I didn't want to go to the Yards. I had to find a way to release Amos. Contlay found me. He brought me to Mt. Sinclair. He saved me."

"We could have been a family," Terris said.

"Enough," Shandra said. "Release them or I'll shoot him," she added, spinning to face Terris.

"You wouldn't," Lana said, her heart beating in her chest so fast she thought it would escape. "He's your son."

"Only in name," Shandra said, her eyes darting to Terris. "I never wanted to have children. You were a mistake. Then you were born covered. You may not know this," she added, looking at Lana. "That's a sign of weakness."

What Alderic told them was true. She hoped, for her friend's sake, that he had been lying. That Shandra and Amos wanted their son, and hadn't willingly offered him as a sacrifice to the demons.

"What about Alderic?" she asked. "Obviously you're not releasing them for him. What do you think he'll do to you when he finds out you've forced me to release them?"

"It won't matter," Shandra said, turning to face her, but keeping the gun trained on her son. "I'll have control over the demons. Alderic won't stand a chance against them."

"I don't understand," Lana said, desperately trying to keep her talking. "I thought you were loyal to Alderic?"

Shandra laughed. "He's weak. He allowed himself to be imprisoned. He allowed his top rebels to be imprisoned right along with him. When he escaped, he didn't even try to free Amos. He's a coward!"

Lana's heartbeat pulsed in her ears. She was running out of things to talk about. She tried to think but the adrenaline pulsing through her was making it hard to concentrate.

"Where's Contlay?" Lana asked, hoping he wouldn't be joining them any time soon.

"It seems our small town's been inundated with out of town visitors. Alderic has his suspicions Contlay, and the Crystal, are in Mt. Sinclair. Contlay's been busy rallying our army. Once we have the demons on our side, we'll be unstoppable. We'll free Amos from the Yards. He was right—Contlay knew you would find us. He knew that you would look for the Crystal and come right to us."

Lana noticed movement out of the corner of her eye—Trevor and Nick were running toward Shandra. She wanted to call out for them to stop but was too late. Shandra sensed that something was happening behind her. As she spun around, the two boys leapt on her.

Lana watched helplessly as the gun fired twice. There was a scream and two thuds as they fell to the floor, blood pooling around them. They had both been shot. Shandra straightened shakily, brushing herself off.

"Would either of you like to try anything?" she asked, looking at Lana and Terris. "I'm not in the mood for these games."

Trevor cried out in pain. Lana instinctively began to rush to him but Shandra aimed the gun at her, effectively stopping her. Nick turned over and moved Trevor toward the wall, away from Shandra, while holding his left arm awkwardly. Lana couldn't see where Trevor had been shot.

"Let them go."

"Not a chance. They're not playing very nice."

Lana contemplated running to Terris and teleporting him to Bridian, and then returning for Trevor and Nick, but didn't want to risk Shandra killing them. She tried to think of something, anything to stop Shandra before Contlay came back. But she was running out of options.

She inhaled a few deep breaths and the fog cleared from her head, making room for an idea. She could stop time. She had done it twice before. She knew she could do it now. Even though there wasn't magic in Mt. Sinclair, it was already in her.

But just as fast as the plan materialized, she realized it wouldn't work. She needed to touch those she didn't want to freeze. She was nowhere near Terris, Trevor, or Nick. Leaving them was out of the question. Her mind worked in overdrive, trying to piece together a new plan.

She heard Terris cry out and wheeled around to look at her friend. He was on his knees.

"Let us go," he said. "Why are you doing this? These are my friends. You said you weren't cut out to be my mother, but you can't want me dead."

Shandra frowned at her son. "Honestly, I don't care what happens to you. All I care about is Amos. He doesn't deserve to be in the Yards, and I'll stop at nothing to free him. It's not my fault you're caught in the middle of this. The blame for that lies on your friend here." She nodded at Lana.

"Doesn't *he* care for me?" Terris asked, looking at the floor. "Won't he want to meet me?"

"When I tell him how weak you are, begging me to spare your friends' lives, he won't want anything to do with you either. Now stand up and act like a VanDriesen."

"Leave him alone," Lana called, anger filling her.

"I'm getting very tired of you." Shandra turned on her. "You're just as weak as my son. You've wasted the blessings your father gave you. Look at you!"

Lana was filled with rage. She had never been so mad before. She glared at Shandra, allowing the anger to seep into her. She knew what she had to do and needed it to motivate her.

She closed her eyes to allow the energy of the Crystal to infuse her. In her mind's eye, she saw thick black smoke holding her, seeping into her skin. It was dark energy. It was the only way she would be able to break it. She had no doubts this time. She knew she could do it. She was strong enough to do it.

A breeze flew through her hair. The demons were restless. They wanted to be released. She knew that once she broke the Crystal, she would have a short window of time to send them back to where they came from. She wasn't sure how she was going to do it, but had to try something to stop the madness around her. Too many people were hurt because of her and the

Crystal. She had to destroy it once and for all before Contlay, or Alderic, figured out how to release the demons without her.

When she felt no more energy from the Crystal, she opened her eyes. Everyone was watching her. She smiled when Shandra began shaking her head in fear, having figured out her plan. She looked at her friends one last time, knowing it may be her last time seeing them.

Lana faced the wall behind the desk and ignored the demons' wailing. She threw the Crystal in the air, keeping her right hand out in front of her. She focused all the energy from her hand and shot it at the Crystal on instinct. She watched it hit the wall and shatter into tiny pieces. The room was no longer light, but filled with a thick black cloud. Shandra gasped as the shapeless demons swarmed the room.

Lana struggled to bring forth any remaining energy deep within her body. She took a moment to steady her breathing and clear her head. The thick black cloud of demons had enveloped the room and she concentrated on them. She cast all doubt aside, knowing that she had to remain calm if she wanted her plan to work. She had never felt so tired and weak in her life, but kept her attention focused on them, willing them closer so she could send them away as one.

Out of the corner of her eye, she saw Shandra advancing. She wouldn't be able to fight her off as well. Suddenly, Terris pushed Shandra to the ground.

Lana let out a tiny breath of relief and fixated on the task at hand. She saw the cloud of demons approaching, and held her hands out, ready to release the dark magic she took from the Crystal. She closed her eyes, wishing that when she reopened them, she would be safe in Bridian. When she reopened them, the black cloud was even closer. Her legs trembled.

The wind picked up, blowing her hair across her face, causing her to lose focus. She heard the demons' shrieking and her stomach recoiled. Trevor was lying on the floor covered in blood. Nick and Terris were trying to subdue Shandra as she waved the gun in the air wildly.

Without any warning, the cloud of demons flew at Lana. She heard their evil laughter and ducked, falling on the floor. The demons dissolved into the thick black mist again, surrounding her completely. The mist seeped into her skin, traveling up her nose, and into her ears. She screamed in pain as it clouded her head and darkness overtook her vision.

After what seemed like hours, the pain subsided, and her vision returned. Shandra was aiming the gun at her son, ready to pull the trigger. Lana held her hands out; a strong wind whipped around her, threatening to topple her. She was standing in the middle of a whirlwind. Nick lay on top of Trevor, holding him to the ground. Terris was pinned against a wall from the force of the wind.

Shandra attempted to throw herself at Lana. When the wind pushed her back to the floor, she had to crawl, digging her nails into the carpet and drawing blood. The wind shifted, lifting her off the floor and pushing her against the wall; her moans lost in the windstorm as it increased in intensity.

All around Lana, her friends screamed. She directed the wind, raising a large cabinet, and let it crash on Shandra. The effort from this overtook her vision again. It was if someone had turned out the lights, leaving her in a dark box. She heard her friends yelling one last time before she succumbed to the darkness.

16

THE AFTERMATH

Lana found herself in her bedroom in Bridian. She couldn't tell how much time had passed. She sat up and found a glass of water on her nightstand and eagerly reached for it. Her mouth was so dry it felt as if a thick film had grown over her tongue. She drank in big gulps, grateful that it was still cold.

When she finished the water, she placed the empty glass back on the nightstand and leaned against the headboard. A sharp ache pierced her forehead, right above her eyes and she pinched the bridge of her nose, hoping to relieve the pressure when everything hit her. She remembered finding the Crystal in Mt. Sinclair. The cabinet pinning Shandra. Her friends being shot. Worst of all, releasing the demons.

The door opened. She saw her parents. For a moment, she didn't move. Was she imagining them? Were they really here?

Jacqueline ran to her. She flung her arms around her, squeezing her tight. "How long have you been up?"

"I just woke up," Lana answered, burying her head in her mother's hair. "You're okay? You're really here?"

Jacqueline stepped back to look at her. Grayson joined them.

"We're really here," he said.

"Did you leave the water for me?"

Jacqueline nodded. "I've been so worried. You've been asleep for so long."

"How are you feeling?" Grayson asked, watching her carefully.

Lana didn't know how to answer, so she said the first thing that came to her. "Tired."

"Why don't you lie back down?" Jacqueline said, pulling the blankets over her.

The questions flew out of Lana. "Where is everyone? Is Trevor all right? Nick? They were shot. It was Shandra."

"Everyone's fine," Jacqueline answered as Grayson pulled up a chair and sat down. "Trevor was shot in the leg. He lost a lot of blood but is recuperating nicely. He's down the hall. Nick was shot in the arm. He is okay."

"Trevor's here?" she asked, glad that she would get a chance to see her friend. "How did he get here?"

"They were able to bring you back to the house," Grayson added. "Damarius found you there and brought you back."

"But why was Trevor brought here?" she asked, trying to unlock the memories that weren't even there. "Why didn't he go home?"

"I think he may be staying here for a while," Jacqueline said, choosing her words carefully.

Lana couldn't help but smile at that, but it didn't take long for her smile to turn into a frown. "What about his mom?"

"She wasn't home or at work," Grayson said. "Damarius couldn't just leave him to recover by himself."

"It's all right, honey." Jacqueline took her hand in hers. "We'll get in touch with Heidi."

"How's he taking everything?" she asked.

Grayson frowned. "He's glad he's not alone. We already talked to King Ramos and he agreed that Trevor can stay here as long as he needs to."

A flash of black crossed her vision. She blinked and it disappeared.

"Are you sure you're feeling all right?" Jacqueline asked. "I swear I saw your eyes turn black for a second."

Lana remembered the flash of black cross her eyes when she broke the Crystal. What was wrong with her? She remembered the demons going inside of her. Were they still there?

"I broke the Crystal," she began. "I couldn't send them back. They went inside me."

"We know." Grayson sighed. "We were able to piece together what happened with Terris and Nick's help."

"What's wrong with me? Is it them? How can I get them out of me?"

"Don't worry," Grayson reassured her. "We just need some time to figure out what our next step should be. You shouldn't have gone by yourself."

"You've always been impulsive," Jacqueline added. "You need to slow down, think before you act. This has all been an adjustment. You can do better. You can *be* better. Trust that we all have your best interests at heart and are doing everything we can to help."

Lana sat up. "I didn't even know if you were alive."

Jacqueline wiped a tear from her eye. She clasped her hands in her lap and gazed out the window.

"We didn't know if you were alive either," Grayson countered.

Lana breathed deeply, trying to suppress her tumultuous emotions.

"When we were attacked," Jacqueline's voice quivered, "all I wanted to do was find you. I shouldn't have left. I knew the soldiers needed help with the luggage, even King Ramos was helping. It shouldn't have happened."

"Is everyone okay?" Lana asked. "Grant?"

Jacqueline buried her face in Grayson's cloak. Lana's mind raced. Had something happened to him?

"Grant's fine," Grayson said. "A few soldiers weren't as lucky. Rebels came upon us so fast. We didn't have time. There were so many of them."

"We lost five," her mother added. "Ander died saving my life. He stepped in front of me. He pushed me away from one of them."

Lana remembered meeting Ander—Bridian's youngest soldier. He was... *had been* only been eighteen. She closed her eyes and felt the tears begin to well up. She cried for Ander. She cried for the lives lost.

"How's Terris?" Lana wiped the tears from her puffy eyes. "Was Shandra captured? Is she in the Yards?"

Her parents exchanged a look, silently debating how to give her bad news. When they didn't answer she assumed the worst.

"She escaped?"

"Honey," Jacqueline said, a pained look on her face. "Shandra's dead."

Why were they upset? She looked at her parents, her eyes wide in fear as the truth hit her.

"Did I kill her?"

"No," Jacqueline shook her head. "From what I gather, a cabinet flew at her. It pinned her to the wall."

"I did that," she said. "The demons... the wind... it was me."

"She was going to kill you," Grayson said. "You did what you had to in the moment."

"Terris," she said in a daze. "He must hate me. I killed his mother."

Lana began crying again. She was tired and defeated. She

had crossed a line that she could never uncross. Her life had irrevocably changed since Mt. Sinclair. No matter what she did, it was permanently tied to her.

Her parents sat with her, holding her hands as she cried. She didn't move or look at them. She kept her gaze straight ahead, knowing how disappointed they must be.

"She was going to kill you," Grayson repeated. "Nick and Terris both told us that. No one blames you. It wasn't even you."

She didn't say anything. She closed her eyes, wishing she could disappear. She didn't care where she went. She just wanted to go and never come back. She was tired of Alderic, Contlay, and the rebels. They were ruining her life and she didn't want the responsibility anymore. She never had.

"Everyone is very anxious to see you," Jacqueline said. "I'm so glad you're okay."

"I'm not. I don't think I ever will be. I can't live like this. I don't understand how it happened. What if they make me do more awful things?"

"You're strong," Jacqueline said, squeezing her hand again. "And you don't have to go through this alone. We're all here for you."

The door opened and Ramos appeared. Lana braced herself for his disapproval. She had endangered not only her life, but Terris, Nick, and Trevor's as well.

"You're up." He sighed with relief.

"I'm sorry. I'm sorry I snuck out. I'm sorry I took Nick and Terris with me. I'm sorry I told Deliah and Dominic not to tell anyone. Please don't be mad at them."

"I'm not mad at them," Ramos said. "I'm not mad at you either. I know why you did what you did. I only wish you had waited."

She wished that she had waited. Maybe things would have ended differently. Ramos could have helped her with the Crystal. If she had his help, maybe the demons wouldn't be inside her.

"Did you share your news?" Ramos asked, looking at her parents.

Jacqueline bit her lip nervously and Grayson took her hand. Lana watched them, wondering what news Ramos was talking about.

"Not yet," Grayson said.

"I don't know if this is the best time," Jacqueline added.

Ramos clasped his hands in front of him, looking sheepish. What were they keeping from her?

"Tell me what?" she asked, looking at her parents, noticing that they were still holding hands.

Neither of them said anything so she stared at Ramos, waiting for him to tell her. He had deep bags underneath his eyes. He looked so tired, so worn out from life. Lana felt a sinking feeling in the pit of her stomach, recognizing that this was her future. When she became Queen of Bridian, she had the same exhaustion to look forward to.

"Oh, come on. Will someone tell me? I can handle it. I think I've been through enough to prove that."

"It's nothing, really." Jacqueline brushed her off.

"I'm sorry I brought it up," Ramos added.

"Something's obviously wrong."

"Nothing's wrong," Jacqueline said, then looked at Grayson. "In fact, it's good news. We're getting married."

Had she misheard? She watched them, looking for a clue, something to let her know she heard correctly.

"We're getting married," Jacqueline repeated when Lana didn't say anything. "When we stopped pretending to be married, we realized just how much we really do love and care for each other. After the attack, we understood there was no use pretending. Life is too short. Each day is a gift and we shouldn't waste it."

Lana looked at her father, waiting for him to tell her they were only joking. "Seriously?"

"Yes," he said.

"That's great!" she exclaimed. "Why didn't you want to tell me?"

"It's not that we didn't want to tell you," Grayson answered. "It just didn't seem like the right time."

"You've been through a lot," Jacqueline added. "There's still more you have to tell us. Damarius could only tell us what little he knew."

"But this is great news," Lana said, sitting up. "I'm so happy for you!"

She was glad they had found happiness. Now she had to find hers.

"I'd like you to be my Maid of Honor," Jacqueline said, watching her hopefully, as if afraid that she would say no. "If you want to."

Lana grinned. "I would love to."

"Well," Ramos said. "I guess we should let you get some more rest."

Her parents stood. They scrutinized her, silently debating if they should leave her alone.

"I'm fine."

"We'll bring you dinner in a while," Jacqueline told her, brushing a section of hair out of her face. "We'll eat with you."

"That would be nice. Can I see Trevor?"

"He's down the hall," Ramos said. "Grant will walk you to his room. I know your cousins are anxious to see you too. I'll let them know you're awake."

Lana got out of bed and swayed when the room began to spin. She had stood up too fast and took a moment to get her bearings. When the room stopped spinning, she saw that Ramos and her parents were looking at each other, concern on their faces.

"I'm fine."

She walked past them into the hall. The last thing she wanted was their pity. When she saw Grant she stopped walking.

"About time you woke up," he said.

Lana ran to him. She wrapped her arms around his waist, hugging him. She was glad that he had survived. He chuckled and she looked up at him.

"We were all so worried about you," he said. "We didn't know what happened to you, where you were."

Another tear slid down her cheek and she brushed it away.

"I bet I know where you're going," he said before leading her to an open door a few feet from her room.

Trevor was propped up in bed, his left leg resting on a pile of pillows. She was so excited to see her friend that she ran to the bed and hugged him. She tried to push the image of him lying on the floor, screaming in pain and covered in blood, out of her mind.

"I've been so worried about you," Trevor said.

"I'm fine," she said. "How are you?"

"The bullet made a clean pass. It'll heal. I'll probably have some trouble walking, but I'm alive."

"I'm so sorry," she whispered. "This is my fault."

"No, it's not." He shrugged. "I wanted to come with you."

There were footsteps behind her and Nick appeared. He had a sling over his right shoulder, where he had been shot. She looked back at Trevor. Why had he been in Trevor's room? They had never been friends. In fact, he used to pick on Trevor just as much as he picked on her.

"Are you okay?" she asked, subtly pointing her head in Nick's direction.

"Relax," Nick spoke up. "We were only talking."

She turned to face him. What else did he want? She brought him to Mt. Sinclair in hopes that he would stay there with his father. She hoped she would never have to see him again.

"He was filling me in on what it's like to live here," Trevor said. "No one can find my mom so it looks like I'm staying here for a while."

"Where do you think she is?" Lana asked.

He shrugged. "She works a lot. Ever since Dad left, she's been struggling to keep us afloat. That much I know."

"I'm sure she's fine." Lana squeezed his hand.

She thought it was odd that his mom had vanished. She knew something was wrong, and the look on her friend's face betrayed that he was worried as well.

"Well, I'm going to go lay down," she said, not wanting to be in Nick's presence any longer, or upset her friend with talk of his missing mother. "I'm still tired. I'll visit you later."

When Trevor nodded she turned to leave, but Nick stopped her.

"Can I talk to you?" he asked, looking at everything but her.

Lana crossed her arms over her chest. All she wanted to do was be alone. She didn't want to talk to him. She had been through so much the last few days. Couldn't he see now wasn't the time?

"What do you want?"

He seemed taken aback by her directness and didn't answer at first. He stared at the ground. In all the years she had known him he had never acted like this before.

"Can we talk alone?" he added.

She stepped into the hallway, wondering what he could possibly want to talk about. Grant led them back to her bedroom. They were silent, adding to the awkwardness.

Nick looked around her room nervously. "I wanted to apologize."

She narrowed her eyes. Had she heard right? This was the last thing she had been expecting. She sat on the edge of her bed before she fell over from shock. She didn't think she would ever see the day that Nick would apologize to her.

"For what?" she asked cautiously.

"For everything." He ran his free arm through his hair. "I know I've been a jerk to you and your friends, and I wanted to tell you that I'm sorry."

Lana scoffed.

"I'm serious," he added. "After everything that happened... I just feel the need to change."

She was quiet. She still didn't believe what he was saying. He had been so mean to her over the years. She looked at him, trying to detect anything that would tell her that he wasn't being sincere.

"That's all I wanted," he said. "I really am sorry."

"Wait." When Nick turned around to look at her, she said, "Did you find your dad?"

"He's here. He was on his way when we went to Mt. Sinclair. He wasn't happy. He missed us, I guess."

Deliah burst into the room, followed by Terris. Nick said something to him that she couldn't hear over Deliah's excitement.

"You're awake!" she squealed.

Dominic joined them a moment later and Nick left. Lana closed her eyes, bracing herself from Deliah's energy. It was all too much.

"Del, give her a minute," Dominic said.

Lana opened her eyes, her gaze stopping on Terris. When his eyes met hers she said, "I'm so sorry."

His face was red and she knew he had been crying. She felt awful and hoped that one day he would be able to forgive her.

"There's nothing you could have done," he said a moment later. "What matters is we're safe."

"Kiernan's been asking about you," Deliah interrupted,

watching Lana from the corner of her eyes. "He came back a few hours ago."

Her cheeks flushed. She looked at her quilt of blue daisies. She didn't want to talk to her cousin about Kiernan in front of Terris and Dominic and hoped she would take the hint and drop the subject. But of course, she didn't, or didn't care, and went on about how many times he had asked about her. She ignored her cousin and focused on Terris, wishing she could think of something comforting to tell him. She decided to let it go until they were alone.

"Is Kiernan's father here? Is he safe?"

"He's here," Terris answered.

Ramos walked into the room and smiled at his children. "You should be downstairs for dinner. Your mother's waiting for you."

"Right," Deliah muttered under her breath.

Lana said goodbye to her cousins and Terris. An older man, wearing a grey cloak joined them, pushing a cart. Weren't her parents eating with her?

When Ramos saw the look on her face he said, "Grayson and Jacqueline will be up shortly."

The man placed the cart in front of her bed. He lifted the lids and stepped back.

"Thank you," Ramos said. "This is all we need."

Ramos handed Lana a plate. She bit her lip, deliberating if her uncle had another reason for eating with her. She pushed the food around her plate absentmindedly.

"I wanted to tell you what Damarius found at the Bureau," he said.

There it was. She set her fork back on her plate, waiting for him to continue. She reached for her water and took a big sip, hoping that would help ease her impatience.

"He spoke to the Director," Ramos said. "As you can understand, we're all upset that Shandra was able to infiltrate them so easily and for so long."

She nodded.

"We went through everything she had stored there. Besides a stack of forged documents, we found pictures of you. She had been watching you for years."

"That's really scary," she said, more to herself than Ramos. "Why was she watching me?"

"Well, she was working with Contlay. We already knew that he was waiting for you to take him to the Crystal."

Ramos looked away, toward the door. A moment later, he looked back at her.

"There may be another reason she had been watching you, but before I say anything, I need to ask you something."

She gazed at him expectantly. Her mind went into overdrive, thinking of all the possible ways the conversation could go.

"If there was a way to take it away, would you want to?"

Lana's forehead furrowed. "Take what away?"

"The magic he infused you with. If there was a way to remove it, to take it away, would you want to pursue that option?"

She didn't even have to think about it. She immediately nodded. She just wanted to be normal. She wanted Terris to have his magic back.

"Damarius found scores of notes belonging to Shandra and Contlay. Amos thought it was possible to take the magic away, to transfer it to themselves. That's probably another reason why Contlay wanted to keep close to you."

"Do you think it's possible?" she asked, her mind working in overdrive.

"I don't know. It's a possibility we never thought of. If the magic can be transferred into you, then I don't see why it can't be transferred out of you. Same with the demons. I need time to figure out if it can be done safely."

"The notes didn't say anything about that?"

Ramos shook his head. "No, they didn't. I'll petition the Council to see if we can question Amos. It will take some time, so I need you to be patient."

"Where would it go?" she asked. "I mean, if we could do it, where would the demons go?"

He shrugged. "That's why I need more time, to figure that out."

"Thank you for telling me," she said, grateful that her uncle had shared this with her.

Lana thought of everything she had been through the past month. How many times her life had been in danger. How many times her friends' lives had been in danger. The thought of one day ruling a land she hardly knew overtook her.

Suddenly, everything came pouring out of her. Tears streamed down her cheeks. A moment later, her sadness turned to anger. She was angry that Alderic had done this to her, to her family. Her hands clenched together, her fingernails digging into the skin.

Ramos reached for her hands. "Be strong, Lana."

"I'm so angry," she said, gritting her teeth. "He did this to me. He ruined my life."

"It's okay to be angry," he said, smiling weakly. "What's not okay is holding onto it, letting it destroy you."

She steadied her breathing. She hoped that she could be strong. She had never imagined that breaking the Crystal would have such a profound consequence on her life.

"I want you to remember that we all have our own demons to face," he added, watching Lana. "Yours are just more literal."

She traced the outline of a daisy, her finger following the blue border. Her uncle reached down and picked something off the floor.

"Why didn't you finish this?"

She looked up, surprised to see her lesson notebook. She sighed, thinking of her unfinished assignment. What was her purpose? Now that she had destroyed the Crystal, she still wasn't any closer to finding an answer.

"I don't think I have a purpose."

Ramos set the notebook next to her. "You're a bright light. You fight for what you believe in, you speak for those who can't, or won't. You inspire others—you're a leader. You may not see it now, but you're going to make a great Queen."

Was she a leader? She had never thought of herself as one. She picked up the notebook and looked at the page. *What is my purpose* was written at the top. The rest of the page was blank.

"Your purpose is to inspire change—provide hope. You were willing to risk your life to help your friends. You're one of the strongest people I know." He stood up. "You'll get through this. Just keep hope. Hope that Alderic and Contlay will go to the Yards and the Rebellion will fall apart without them. The Council has their best reapers searching for them."

She bit her lip. While it was nice to hear, she didn't believe it. She didn't feel like a leader and wondered if she ever would.

"When we were looking for the Crystal, I heard the demons. They were so loud, but Terris couldn't. Do you know why that was?"

He looked away. "I assume it's because of the magic. The dark magic Alderic infused you with drew them to you, left you more susceptible, more aware of them."

"When I picked it up, it burned my skin. It didn't do that the first time I touched it, when I found it in the fireplace."

Ramos was quiet for a moment, and then answered. "The longer you're in Bridian, the stronger you're becoming. You siphon magic from around you, out of the air itself. The demons were probably drawing your magic, which in turn heated it. But that's only a guess. We may never know the answer."

She looked away but something else had been plaguing her. "Did you know I'm connected to Terris?"

Her gazed drifted back to her uncle, trying to read his reaction.

"Yes." He looked to the floor. "I know Alderic's plan was to kill him. He connected you to make you stronger. Since they were interrupted before Terris was killed, it makes sense you're connected in some way."

Lana frowned. She didn't really understand what that meant, or how it affected their friendship, but knew it was significant.

"Grayson and Jacqueline should be up soon with dessert. I believe it was chocolate cake tonight."

"Thanks," she said, genuinely happy that she had family to support her, when she thought of the drawings again.

"Wait, Uncle Ramos," Lana called. "Why do you think Damon drew the Welcome Center? Why were they at Poklin's?"

"I hate to say it, but my son is a rebel. He must have realized the Welcome Center was an extension of the Bureau. He probably drew it when he went to see Contlay. Maybe he even drew it for my brother. He must have lost them in Poklin's."

She watched him leave, remembering Shandra's comment about Mt. Sinclair being inundated with out of town visitors. Rebels. They had been looking for Contlay and the Crystal. For a moment she wondered what would have happened if she hadn't found Damon's drawings. If they hadn't been left behind in Poklin's, if Damon had remembered the Welcome Center, Alderic may have found the Crystal.

She hoped that her parents wouldn't take long. She didn't want to be left alone. As she scanned her bedroom, her crown caught her attention. She walked to the dresser and placed it on her head. She looked at her reflection in the mirror when the darkness swam across her eyes again, blocking her vision.

She clutched the dresser and closed her eyes. When the feeling passed, she looked in the mirror again, surprised to see the irises of her eyes were black. For the first time since returning to Bridian she felt strong, powerful even, and her lips curved into a smile.

Her parents joined her, cake in hand. She glanced in the mirror again, watching her eyes return to brown. She wondered how long she had until the demons overtook her once and for all before turning to her parents, a forced smile on her face.

ALSO BY JESSICA LEMORE

The Mirrored Crown Series (Young Adult Fantasy)

The Princess of the Rebellion

The Crystal of Medora

The Darkness Within

The Shadow Marked Series (New Adult Fantasy Romance)

Curse of Lies and Shadow

Curse of Darkness and Desire: Coming Soon

If you've enjoyed this book, please leave a review!

ABOUT THE AUTHOR

Jessica R. LeMore is the author of *The Mirrored Crown* series. She lives in Upstate New York with her husband and son. You can visit her online at www.jessicarlemore.com.

facebook.com/jessicarlemore
x.com/jessicarlemore
instagram.com/jessicarlemore

www.ingramcontent.com/pod-product-compliance
Lightning Source LLC
Chambersburg PA
CBHW070650100726
47907CB00007B/2163